The Thirteenth Man

Feb. 24, 2003

To Pam,

Wishing you the best in this journey,

[signature]

The Thirteenth Man

by Rudy A. Pizarro

Writer's Showcase
New York Lincoln Shanghai

The Thirteenth Man

All Rights Reserved © 2003 by Rudy A. Pizarro

No part of this book may be reproduced or transmitted in any form or by any means, graphic, electronic, or mechanical, including photocopying, recording, taping, or by any information storage retrieval system, without the written permission of the publisher.

Writer's Showcase
an imprint of iUniverse, Inc.

For information address:
iUniverse, Inc.
2021 Pine Lake Road, Suite 100
Lincoln, NE 68512
www.iuniverse.com

ISBN: 0-595-25765-8 (pbk)
ISBN: 0-595-65316-2 (cloth)

Printed in the United States of America

*To honor
Carlos Bulosan
and all the Filipino immigrants in his book
"America is in the Heart"*

PREFACE

The Thirteenth Man is an offshoot of my book *Where True Peace Lies*, a story based on some feeling I had one quiet morning. It was such that it touched me in my inmost self, and made me wonder what it was and what it meant. But my mind went blank and I felt "lost like a goose in a tall grass."

Was it a spiritual feeling? I asked. I started reading up. The grass cleared and I saw Him. "This way," he said. He *leadeth* me and I followed him—and that made all the difference in me.

I thought a novel would give more breadth and depth to my story. I feel *The Thirteenth Man* had done that but, on second thought, I let the reader be the judge.

INTRODUCTION

So a prophecy was told: *Then I, Daniel, looked and saw two men on each bank of a river. And one of them asked the man in a linen robe who was standing now above the water, "How long will it be until all terrors end?"*

He replied with both hands lifted to heaven, taking oath by him who lives forever and ever, that they will not end until three and a half years after the power of God's people are crushed.

I heard what he said but I didn't understand what he meant, so I said, "Sir, how will this all come out?"

But he said, "Go now, Daniel, for what I have said is not to be understood until the time of the end. Many shall be purified by great trials and persecutions. But the wicked shall continue in their wickedness, and none of them will understand. It will not be understood until the end times, when travel and education shall be vastly increased. And even then only those who are willing to learn will know what it means."

So the wicked continue in their wickedness. They continue to ignore the warnings by the prophets from Abraham to Moses to Isaiah and Daniel, and get punished over and over again. They keep defying God's laws. They are stubborn and rebellious. Why? They did not understand something. *Even now when the Scripture is read it seems as though their hearts and minds are covered by a veil, because they cannot see and understand the real meaning of the Scriptures. Yes, even today when they read Moses' writings their hearts are blind and they think that obeying the Ten Commandments is the way to be saved. The veil of misunderstanding can be removed only by believing in Christ.*

What is the meaning of the prophecy? Who is Christ? How does one believe? The answers lie in the questions asked by a little girl: "What is that I see? Is the star winking at me?"

* * * *

The Thirteenth Man is a story about Dan, a modern man, who would devote his life telling the world what he learned from the little girl—and how.

"Can I call you the Thirteenth Apostle?" asked the newsman.

"No," Dan replied, humbly. "I neither walk, broke bread nor shared wine with the Man. Call me, perhaps, the Thirteenth Man because I share the same Spirit his Apostles had. I'll do what the Apostles did—spread the Word of the Lord but with an added meaning."

"What's that?" asked the newsman.

"Nature, of course," Dan replied.

Chapter 1

▼

Skill and luck made Dan a poker Midas who turned cards into gold. Poker made him a multi-millionaire. He was only in his twenties.

He embarked on his new career when he started playing in a lowly 3-5 dollar game in LA. He quickly fell in love with poker. He loved the freedom and the chance to make big money. He loved the aura of the rugged, individualist cowboy. He loved the gentlemanly combat of nerve and skill. He figured that if poker is, indeed, a game of skill he could become one of its best shooters, if not the best, and the best would wind up with all the money. After a long winning streak, he quit his job as an insurance salesman and became a professional poker player.

Dan went up the money ladder fast when he won a series of local tournaments and then the biggest—the million-dollar bonanza in Las Vegas. He became big time. Now, he said, he would play anyone in any amount he could count in any poker game he could name. He had minted a new name for himself—the "Golden Boy."

* * * *

Golden Boy Dan moved to Las Vegas soon after winning the million-dollar. He knew Las Vegas would be where the action is. It is where he could catch a whale. Just to be ready when he shows up, he put the bulk of his money in the Poker Room's safe deposit box. He also left his phone number to call anytime.

* * * *

It was George last day in Las Vegas before he had to go back to Seattle. He and his wife Diane were in town for a few days for the annual COMDEX, a convention of entrepreneurs and consumers in the computer field. He is a dot-com millionaire, a Baby Bill (after the founder of Microsoft). He is *the* whale. While Diane loves to shop, George loves poker, especially the high-stakes poker. He, too, loves the nerve and mental combat. The money he loses doesn't really matter much to him, given his tremendous wealth. Yet, he would ask himself why he threw money away instead of giving it to charity, several of which he supports.

George had played with Dan a few times in a ring game before, losing the pot to him every time he went up against him. He helped fatten Dan's bankroll considerably. But he was not discouraged. He loved the challenge, and he knew he would catch Dan one of these days. He had a strategy.

* * * *

Dan's cell phone rang. It was the Poker Floor Supervisor, informing him that George had just walked in.

"I'll be right there," Dan said, feeling a surge of excitement. He happened to be at the Mirage at the time, at the CPK, where he was just finishing off a dish of ravioli. He'd park his Mercedes there then walked the couple of blocks to the Bellagio to play. He loved the brisk walk. He loved Las Vegas. He admired the guts, ingenuity and industry of the men who built it. He admired the genius who invented poker. He thought they are the natural expressions of man's innate talent when free to act. It is freedom the American way, he thought. It was also his way.

The walk burned away his calories, too, so that, with his usual workouts in a fitness club, he looks athletic. Moreover, it gave him time to prep, as he ran through his mind the strategies he would use against any opponent. He had diligently kept a portfolio of notes on them: their "tells," strengths and weaknesses, where and how they live and even tidbits about their wives and children. This time he focused on George, on whom he kept the most detailed notes. So now, he would meet him. He would battle the whale head-to-head. This is *the* chance of a lifetime, he thought. The Golden Boy was ready.

* * * *

"Hi, George! Hi, Diane! Dan said in greeting, as he stepped up the raised floor of the high-roller area. He shook George's hand and then touched cheeks with Diane. "How long you gonna be in town for?" he asked George.

"Been here coupla of days—gotta go back tonight," George said. "I thought I'd stop by for some fun."

The table was ready—dealer, box and the decks. They seated at opposite ends, their chips and cash in front of them. Diane sat next to George. The word went around and the railbirds gathered along the rails to watch.

* * * *

A few hours into the game, Dan was ahead two-hundred thousand. They were playing a $1,000,000 dollar-buy-in, $2,000-$4,000 limit Hold-Em with $1,000 and $2000 blinds. All of sudden, George suggested they changed to No-Limit, with the same blinds. Dan wondered why, but he welcomed it. "This is it! Showdown time!" he thought, excitedly.

George bought two-million more in personal check, which cleared promptly. Now, he had in front of him $2,800,000 in $10,000, $5,000 and $1,000 chips. Dan had a total $2,750,000, after emptying a boxful of cash and chips.

For a while, Dan had the upper-hand. He was playing with intensity, yet relaxed and focused. He was well-known for his uncanny analysis of his opponent's play and an almost phenomenal memory and knowledge of odds. He could almost pinpoint with accuracy his opponent's hand. Besides, he was running lucky.

At least up till then when, suddenly, like a lightning out of the blue, catastrophe struck. He was hit by a miracle draw when another deuce turned up on the river and everything he had went to George.

Dan was stunned. His heart sunk. "He called me all the way with that?" he murmured in utter disbelief. He saw George had only two outs, but he knew him all too well. Give him a one-outer and he would stick with you all the way. George did it to him many times before but he lost each time. But he came to play, and this time he beat Dan. And not only that—he outright busted him. Now Dan could only stare at all that money. "Why?" he asked, as if pleading for mercy or a second chance. "Why didn't I move all in to scare him away before or on the flop? Why didn't I…?"

* * * *

What busted Dan was a pair of black Aces in the hole. George had the small blind. He called the big blind. Dan sweetened the pot with twenty-thousand. George called. As usual, George wanted to see the flop, which turned up to be *K, 2, 6,* of spades, clubs and diamonds. Dan, as usual, did his analysis of the board. The hand that could beat his at that stage was a set or two pairs. Whatever draw George had wasn't threatening. He then bet out $200,000, to feel George out or scare him away. But George didn't run away. Instead, he raised him fifty thousand! Dan asked why, and why just that amount. He concluded that, as usual, George raised—not on the strength of his hand—but to feel him out, too. Dan also knew that if George had a set or two pairs he would have just called. He was pretty sure he got him that point. Dan just called, thinking of a larger payoff down the river. The turn card was a *nine* of hearts, giving another possible set, two pairs and a straight draw. He looked at George and saw no sign of strength, as would be indicated by his tell. Not a trace of emotion stirred in him. The same guileless and innocent expression was on his face. This tell had earned Dan thousands from him before. He knew George wouldn't back off now. Dan pushed all his stacks in. George eyed the pot like a fish to a lure. Sure enough, he called and pushed everything he had in front of him.

Perfect! Beautiful! I got him!" Dan gloated, as he stared at the monstrous pot—$5,500,000 all in all! He already thought it was his. Then the river card came. Another *deuce*! Dan's heart leaped. Thinking he had the best hand, he turned up his cards. What he saw, however, was just a mirage, when George turned up his hand and showed an ace of diamonds and a deuce of hearts, to give him three deuces with an ace kicker—and won the pot! But George didn't whoop it up as he dragged the pot in. Instead, he felt guilty when he saw the pain in Dan's face. He thought Dan's entire money was all in the pot. He is that kind of man who feels guilty when he wins and feels guilty when he loses.

* * * *

The pot should have belonged to Dan by right—by his skill and courage and years of diligent study. He thought poker was a game of skill, and he was the master, at least according to his admirers. But what comes around goes around, so the prophetic saying went. Skill, knowledge and courage do not go around but Luck does. This time, Luck went to the fish, a recreational player, playing almost blindfolded and hit the pot. This time, the fish swallowed the fisherman.

But George did not feel triumphant. So he won a couple million bucks. So what! he thought. He wanted to say something to salve Dan, but he had left before he could say it.

The railbirds couldn't believe it either. It was one hell of a bad beat, they all said. They nodded at Dan in admiration when he came by them. Dan paused to talk to his friends Pete and Mat. They shook his hand and patted him on the back. "Well—what goes around comes around. You'll come back," Pete said, trying to comfort his friend.

So what goes around comes around, indeed. There's a season and reason for everything. It was Dan's time to lose. This time, luck fell on George. The reason? George had been playing long enough and rich enough and paying off—and learning or not learning along the way—all the disastrous bad plays he made and all the bad beats and bluffs he had ran into. But he was more than rich enough to last this long, to arrive finally at this particular moment. And what's Dan's reason for sticking around? "Any amount you can count, in any poker game you can name," cockily, he did say. There would be more money down the river, he figured. After all, he'd beaten George so many times before. Now he wished he'd done this or he'd done that. But it was all a pointless wishful thinking now. Now, he was only *chasing the wind*. He was at the *wrong place at the wrong time*. He didn't know he was *going to run into bad luck that day. He is like a fish caught in a net*.

Downcast, Dan walked back to the Mirage, unaware of the crowd and the countless neons that flashed just as relentlessly as the huge pot that flashed in his head and tortured him.

He drove home to his luxurious condo located in a gated community several miles away, half-conscious of the cars that cut him, and the guard that greeted him as he passed through. He was driving a gleaming black SL 600 that he bought new, along with the condo, when he made the big hit. He had the Life of the Rich financed with Easy Money. It was an adrenalin-filled lifestyle. But now, he had no more. Now he felt the exact reverse. He was sick. He went straight to the liquor cabinet and took out a bottle of whiskey and a pocket of cocaine. He knocked himself out to sleep.

*   *   *   *

Dan awakened with a jolt in the middle of the night. The liquor and drug had worn off. The fear and confusion that had wracked his soul earlier came back even more intensely. He talked to himself. "Why?...What did I do wrong?...I shouldn't have played that god-damned No-Limit...I shouldn't have left all my money in the box...How could I be so stupid?...Damn that bastard!...He cold-decked me for over five million bucks!...I should have quit while I was ahead...I wish—" He ran out of drug. He emptied the bottle and knocked himself back to sleep.

*   *   *   *

Dan stirred from his stupor to pick up the phone that kept ringing.

"Hi, honey?" Betty said. "How you feelin'? Pete said you had a real bad day yesterday. But could you make it to the party tonight? Could you come over to—"

Brusquely, Dan cut her off: "Leave me alone, okay?"

"That bad, eh?" Betty retorted and slammed the phone down. Dan was supposed to meet her at Caesar's for lunch and pick up an evening dress with her.

Dan didn't feel like eating, but he forced himself to a three-day old leftover pizza. Gone would be the 5-Star menu that includes caviar hors d'oeuvres and the finest wines. He wouldn't be at the party that night or in the cruise to the Virgin Islands next week. He looked around his kitchen then outside to the velvety, manicured lawn, then into his richly-furnished living room. They looked differently now. He noticed the pile of bills on the table. They were due. He only had a few grand in his checking account. For personal reason, he didn't make any investment or saved in the bank. All his money was in that poker box. He kept a box at home where he'd stash away a few bundles but those, too, were in that box.

He knew he would be losing his home and Mercedes. He knew he could get more money for them if he could take his time, but he didn't have much time. He had to act fast.

He never had to worry before. Just a day's win would take care of everything. Now he was desperate. He considered borrowing money from Pete or Mat—or borrow and don't pay, which sometimes happens among gamblers; or borrow from his dad, but he knew he didn't have much to give. Thoughts of the millions and how he lost them stabbed him again and again. "Damn!" he swore, slamming his fist on the table. He gobbled up the pizza and shoved it down with a swig then went back to bed.

* * * *

The glare of the afternoon sun hit Dan in the face and woke him up. He edged over the bed and picked up the phone to make a call.

"Mat, this is Dan," he drawled, groggily.

"Hi, Pal!" Mat said. "I saw Betty with Pete at the party last night."

"That bitch!" Dan mumbled softly to himself. He pushed the thought away. "I need a few grand, Mat."

"I understand. No problemo," Mat answered. "You wanna use your car for collateral?"

"No. Why—don't you trust me?" Dan asked.

"You're my friend Dan but that's the way I do business. How much do you owe on it?" Mat insisted.

Dan didn't feel like dickering. "About thirty," he said.

"Okay—this is what I'll do," Mat said. "I'll payoff your loan and you sign off the title to me. I'll give you fifteen grand." Dan knew his equity was more than that, but he didn't feel like going around talking to pawn shops or selling it by owner. "The bastard doesn't trust me," he murmured. Dan had loaned money to others before but he never asked for collateral. He had a list of them. And, except for one, the "loans" were never paid back. But he needed the money now—and a transportation.

"I gotta have transportation," Dan said.

"I'll give you mine," Mat said.

"Good enough," Dan said. He planned to use part of the money to take care of the bills but not the condo, which he planned to sell right away. With the leftover, he'd add it to the few thousands he had left to play in the smaller limit. A while later, he met Mat at the loan company and signed the papers. Mat paid him in cash. They exchanged keys.

"You gonna be at the Bellagio?" Dan asked, as they walked out the door.

"Yeah," Mat answered, eager to get his hand on the gleaming black Mercedes. He knew he had a steal. "Later tonight," he said.

Dan was not as eager to get his hand on the beat-up Oldsmobile. It was Mat's spare car.

Chapter 2

Dan met Betty after his big win. She worked as a hair stylist and manicurist. She was also in her twenties, single and very attractive—blonde, blue-eyed and petite. On her off-days, she played poker where Dan played. She and Dan, then a bachelor-Golden Boy, were like marquee attractions. She was magnetized to him and he to her. Quickly, they became friends.

They took trips together—to France, Italy, Switzerland, Hawaii and other places. They partied with friends out at sea in cruises and around town. They were inseparable in the eyes of their friends, but they didn't live together. Dan needed privacy for thought and study.

Now he needed her. But Dan didn't want to ask her if he could move in with her. He was sure she wouldn't want him now, sure that she'd tell him she needed her privacy, too, now, with a new boyfriend, with Pete, of course. He thought about his ex-Mercedes and now his ex-girlfriend. He thought about all the fun they had together, all the money he had lavishly spent for her. That was his ex-life. He thought how a turn of a card could change everything in an instant.

* * * *

The locals knew who's in and who's out. They knew that Betty used to go out with Dan. They knew the one hell of a bad beat he had only a few days ago and the reason he was now playing in the lower limit game. They threw furtive glances at him. He wasn't the same trimmed and well-dressed guy they used to know. That night he was hiding himself in a baseball hat, dark glasses and an unshaven face. He was drinking.

Heads turned when Pete and Betty walked into the room. Pete led Betty by the hand as they made their way through the weekend crowd. Dan noticed the curiosity, but he ignored it. His back was towards the entrance. Pete and Betty went by his table. They didn't notice Dan. They stepped up to the raised floor of the poker area, to a loud greeting from a high-roller: "Look-a here! Someone new eh, Pete? Eh, Betty?"

Dan heard it. "That bitch!" he murmured. It rattled him and lost his focus. It hurt him where it counted—his ego, the ego of the Golden Boy. He picked up his chips and left the room. He went to play blackjack where he continued drinking. He lost the rest of his fifteen grand in minutes. He couldn't believe he did it. He knew he had never done that before. He had never acted that impulsively before. But that night he couldn't help himself anymore. He had lost total control of himself. He became more depressed and desperate.

* * * *

Dan paid three-hundred thousand for his condo. He still owed two-hundred fifty thousand. The reason he didn't cash it out was that he could use some "tax shelter" with the interest payments. Now he had to get rid of it. He wanted to use a realtor but he didn't want to spend money on commission. He called Mat again. They made a deal.

Mat gave him twenty grand for his equity and took over his mortgage. The sale included all the furniture and appliances.

Dan gathered his belongings and moved to a budget motel that leased out on a monthly basis. He played in the smaller rooms around the city. He drank as usual while he played. He used comps for meals. One day he had a fight with another player who recognized him. He insulted Dan, calling him a bum after losing a pot to him. Dan punched him in the mouth and knocked him down. He was arrested and charged but the case was dismissed. But he had to hire a lawyer which cost him a couple of grand. He also got barred from the room.

Dan went back into selling insurance. He didn't stay very long, though. He couldn't keep his appointments because of his drinking. He took a job driving cab. But he was fired when he got into an accident due to his fault. He and his company were sued. He was charged with negligent driving and DUI. He got fined. After paying the lawyer's fee, he was flat broke. He was sent to prison for one year. He knew he was getting deeper and deeper into trouble but he couldn't help it.

"How did I get into this mess? Why?" he asked himself, as he stared at the low ceiling of the tiny cell he shared with another inmate. He could see how he got there. Why it happened was a deep dark. His poker discipline couldn't help him; or the prayers his mom taught him when he was little; or the philosophy course he took in college; or his superficial reading of the bible; or his thoughts about God.

He turned philosophical. "Is this God's Will?" he asked. That was even a tougher question. There seemed to be this *veil of misunderstanding* over this God's will thing. "Is it God's will if I went the wrong way because I didn't know any better? Or if I knew better yet chose to go the wrong way because of a temptation—would that still be God's will?" Dan did not have any inkling. It was a philosophical question that he must deal with in deep quietness. This he didn't have. He didn't because his life was a life at the surface. His was like a shallow-rooted tree that got knocked down in a storm.

"Welcome to the 'hood, man," his cell-mate said. Dan ignored him. He wasn't in the mood. The man kicked the bottom of his bunk. "Dya hear me, man?"

"Yeah—I hear you. What a fuck ya want," Dan answered, angrily.

"I'm Trick. Whatya in for?" Trick asked.

"DUI. Hurt somebody. Got one year," Dan said.

"Ain't too bad," Trick said. "Ma'self, I got six years. Dealin' drug. Three to go."

Time stood still for Dan. He'd never been more bored in his life, but at least he got a breathing room. When he was released, Trick gave him a name and a phone number. He also told him he could use his car.

* * * *

With a ticket paid for by a relief agency, Dan took a bus to LA. He was going there to stay with his dad, whom he had not seen since he moved to Vegas. He was now in his advanced years. He lived by himself in a one-bedroom apartment for the elderly. He never re-married after his wife passed away when Dan was still in high school. Dan was their only child. He helped pay for his medical bills when he was hospitalized from a stroke that had hobbled him since then.

He shuffled with a cane to answer the door. He opened it and paused a moment. He thought he was looking at a stranger. He looked thin and unshaven. His clothes needed a cremation rather than a laundry.

"Hi, dad!" Dan said, as he took a step to embrace him.

"Dan! What a surprise!" He said, putting out his free arm.

"Happy to see you, dad," Dan said.

"You look awful, son. You've lost a lot of weight," his dad said. The last time he heard from him, Dan was on a roll. "I've not heard much from you since you left. How've you been?"

"Okay, dad," he said. "For a while, I was doing just great. Then I had this one bad night and I lost everything. I know you told me once, 'if it's worth living for, it's worth fighting for.' Well, I thought it was worth to try double my money, so I went for it and got killed. Then I had a couple scrapes with the law. I didn't want to tell you and worry you, dad. I'm sorry. Need to get on my feet. That's why I'm here. Hope you wouldn't mind. I'm sorry."

"It's okay, son," his dad said. "Glad to have you back."

"This place looks nice," Dan said. "And you look good, too."

"Oh, I manage," his dad said. "Now and then I get help from Jack, my old army buddy."

There was a long pause. A lunch meal was brought in, which they shared.

"Dad, do you have a few bucks on you?" Dan asked.

"I ain't got much, son. My check hasn't come in yet," his dad said, now sure that Dan was really broke.

"Gotta see somebody," Dan said.

* * * *

Dan called the number Trick gave him. Muscle was home. He lived in Compton, a half-way across the city. Dan took a cab.

Dan felt uneasy walking down the block looking for the address. He was conscious of himself, an unshaven white man in sneakers and a baseball hat, the visor out front, suspicious and looking suspicious. He used to drive through there on his way to a poker club.

He knocked on a door. Nobody answered. He noticed a peephole. He knocked again. A large muscular man emerged.

"Hi, I'm Dan."

"Come on in," Muscle said in a deep, throaty voice, as he threw a wary glance up and down the road. He pointed to a worn-out sofa in the living room.

"Here's the deal, man," Muscle said, without so much as introducing himself. Perhaps he knew his muscles spoke more precisely than his words. "I want you to cover the poker rooms—ya understand? This, here, contains ten packets, at two-hundred bucks a pop—ya follow me? Ya get twenty percent cut—ya know what I mean? Ring me up when you need more." He handed Dan a small bag containing plastic packets of the white stuff. He also gave him a key to the car. He gave Dan his phone number and his code name, "Skinny." He provided Dan his own cell phone and also his code name, the initials "LV."

Trick knew Dan would come in handy. He had lived in the area. And as a poker player, he had contacts with the players, especially the high rollers.

Dan had heard so much about the big money being made in drugs. Although he knew it was a risky business, it was the only way he knew of to get rich quick. That evening, shaven and in better clothes, he drove to a poker club. He saw familiar faces in the high-limit section. He walked up to one of them.

"How ya doin' Rod?" Dan said in a low voice, as he stood behind him. Rod wasn't in a hand.

"Look who's here—the Golden Boy!" Rod exclaimed, as he got up to shake Dan's hand. "How've you been, man. I heard what happened."

"Just a temporary setback," Dan said. "How about you?"

"I'm stuck pretty bad right now," Rod said. "Been playing ten hours." Dan knew Rod used coke to get him through nights like this. They had done this together a few times before. They left together and went to the bathroom. Dan slipped him three packets. A man was using the urinal. He recognized Dan, the man who punched him.

Dan went around the room. He ran into two others he knew. They went outside to the parking lot to make the exchange. His phone rang.

"Skinny here. Look-a here, man. You gotta be more discreet—ya understand?"

"Got ya," Dan answered. Muscle knew the area was hot and under constant surveillance. Much had been happening around there lately.

Dan sold all his stuff that night and made a few hundred bucks. He called Muscle for more. They met at a restaurant where, under the table, Dan turned in the money minus his cut. Muscle slipped a bag containing twenty packets. They finished their coffee and sandwich quickly then left. They didn't want to hang around too long.

Dan visited another club. He quickly sold what he had. But this time he made the delivery in a hotel nearby. He was really surprised at how easy it was to make money. Users just craved for it. He got more and more of the stuff and made more and more money. Now he thought of going on his own. He talked to Skinny, who talked to a higher-up. Dan would do the Las Vegas clubs. Muscle would be his under-boss and enforcer.

* * * *

The man in the bathroom called the LA police to report what he saw. A detective met him to take the information. Later on, in his office, the detective forwarded the information to the Metro Police and the FBI in LasVegas. Dan was put under surveillance.

* * * *

Dan was back on his feet. He was back in La Vegas. Now he had a growing platoon of peddlers. He was playing poker again, although in a less-known joint a little way from the strip. He was lying low.

He could sit back and enjoy while the money poured in. He had recouped much of the money he lost to George. He thought about the old days—big-time poker, Betty and all. He considered cutting it and run. Just then his phone rang and broke his rosy reverie.

"Hi, LV. This is SL. Listen. I got somethin' cookin.' This is going to be a real biggie. I'll come down and talk to you. What dya say, eh, pal?"

SL (named after the automobile), was in the higher echelon of the drug ring, the "warehouseman," or the main distributor. If SL says "real biggie," it's a biggie. Dan decided to do it just once then run.

"Common down," Dan answered. "You know where I live."

SL found Dan lolling on lounge chair by the pool, wearing dark sunglasses, with a cigar in his mouth. He kept a classy dig near the strip.

"Listen," SL said. "I got this guy with ecstacy stuff. He wants somebody to supply the strip. You wanna do it?"

"I could do the clubs," Dan said, decidedly. "I'll check things out and let you know."

"Great. We're in business," SL said, patting Dan on the shoulder. "I'll let you finish your sun."

That evening Dan visited a club. It was filled with young revelers. He ordered a drink then introduced himself to the manager. His name was Luke. He told Luke what he had. Luke was interested. He said his crowd would love it. When Dan left, the manager promptly called the cops.

Dan didn't know he was on a hot list that was distributed all over southern Nevada. He wasn't aware that a trap was now being set up for him. The next day, Luke called Dan and invited him to join him for lunch at his club. Dan gladly accepted the invitation. However, he suggested they met at a park, instead.

Luke was wired up by the narcotics agents. He arrived at the park minutes before the agreed time. Unseen from a distance in a new SUV, Muscle and Dan watched him, making sure that nobody was with him. Then they drove up into view.

It was a quick deal. It was worth several hundred grand, which would be paid in cash upon delivery. The stuff would be delivered at 10 p.m. that night by one of Dan's couriers. He would deliver it by the club's back door.

That night, Dan went to play at a big poker game, with Muscle at his elbow. That night a dozen Metro, FBI and Narcotics Agents covered them. A number of unmarked cars were parked outside the two clubs. When the stuff was delivered and verified, and the money exchanged hands, the men swooped down simultaneously, handcuffed Dan, Muscle and the courier, seized the money and drugs and whisked them away.

Dan was tried and convicted. He was sent to the State Penitentiary to do ten years, with a possibility of parole after five. Muscle was sent to a different facility, where he would do fifteen years. He had one previous prior conviction for armed assault. The courier, who testified against Dan and Muscle, was given a light sentence of three years, one year in county jail and the rest on probation. Dan's rosy reverie became a nightmare.

Chapter 3

Dan was crushed mentally and emotionally. The penitentiary is a high-security home for hardened criminals of all stripes. He was in for a real hard time.

To start the day, he and Buster, his cellmate, would be roused by the noise of a baton rattling across the bars. Then they'd get ready for muster before filing out to the mess hall to eat. Then they'd gather in an enclosed courtyard where they would be broken up into gangs then taken to their task for the day.

Dan was assigned to a field crew to load one-or two-man rocks onto trucks. He would be doing this for a certain period of time. This was an eight hour job for which he would be paid ten cents an hour. The job was one of the hardest ones. It was considered a make-or-break job.

Armed guards watched them like hawks. They barked at them for being slow or even when their minds seemed to wander away. They didn't give them time to daydream. They wanted them to focus. Dan realized the purpose of all these and the knowledge helped him coped.

"How did I get into this mess? Why?" Dan asked himself again and again, feeling more remorseful. He began to realize how shallow a person he was. He realized he got into this mess because he couldn't resist the temptation. He was weak because of greed, and greed is not deep and rational. It is not based on conscience, which is something borne way down deep, which is where spirituality lies. He could hold his impulses while he considered a poker move. But in poker he didn't need conscience. Take no prisoners including your own grandma, he'd say. Winning the pot was all that mattered to him, as a saying went: *"Life's but a game, and existence but a quest for profit, and that to make money all is justified, even evil."* This was his attitude. Every pot he raked in added to his true worth as a person and "true worth" to him meant the "good life:" luxury, fame and all the fat trimmings the world offers. If he had had a life that went deeper than that, perhaps he could have heard the voice of his conscience that would have whispered to him not to commit the crime. But, right now, his thoughts and emotions were being swept away by the weight of the rocks that bent his back, ached his muscles and popped sweat down his face. It was telling him *something*.

* * * *

Dan quickly adjusted to life in the hard labor department, where he did three years. The guards started to ease up on him. The detail supervisor assigned him to a soft job—cleaning around the yard and tending to a garden of flowers, shrubs and fruit trees. It was a life on the beach for him. There he was in the soft, bright morning sun or under a shady tree, just listening to the silence.

* * * *

"A beautiful day!" A voice said, breaking the silence.

Dan turned his head and said, "Yes, sir. Just perfect, sir. I was in a different world." He picked up his shovel to continue digging.

"It's okay, son. We can talk a bit. I'm Brother Simeon. I've been observing you."

"I'm Dan, Brother Simeon," Dan answered.

"You know, Dan, the Book of Psalms refers to this beauty and silence of nature. It says: '*He leadeth me by the still water. He comforteth me.*' Jesus also referred to his connection with nature when he said: '*Come ye you yourself into a lonely place and rest a bit…You can't come to me unless the Father attracts you to me.*' What's happening to you right now is that you're being attracted to the Father through his handiwork—the nature here. By 'attract' I mean, you're being touched in the innermost sanctum of your being, that little thing deep inside your heart and mind or your soul, if you will. This is the touch of the Holy Spirit. This Spirit is not just a word or a symbol. It is real. It's as real as the flowers and the trees around you. This feeling is as real. Where else could you get this kind of blissful peace? Nowhere else. Many people think they could get it from a human source—from drugs or alcohol, or from things that money can buy or from a roomful of icons or statues. You get this peace only from nature. This touch is your bond with Him. It is the key to understanding Him and His message of Love. Without this feeling of the Spirit in you, you wouldn't, therefore, have this special bond with Him. In fact, you would misunderstand Him. Let this then be a personal basis of your faith.

Brother Simeon opened a bible and continued: "Just what other things the Spirit could do for you, consider this: '*The Spirit makes the heavens beautiful. Who is wise enough to number the stars? It is not age that makes man intelligent. It is the Spirit that gives intuition and instinct. It is the breath of the Almighty that makes man wise. They do not know where to find wisdom but death and destruction speak of knowing something about it.*' You have suffered, son, so you may learn this thing. But why must you suffer just to learn it when all you could have done was go back to nature? Why? Because you'd lost your childhood innocence and your life became superficial. You became spoiled rotten.

"*It is not age that makes man intelligent.* 'What is that I see? Is the star winking at me?' a little girl asked. As if by a lighted lamp, she and the star saw each other honestly. You were once this child, son. You once had her Spirit. But now you've found it back.'*Unless you turn to God from your sins and become as little children, you will never get to the Kingdom of Heaven.'*

"Jesus talked about the '*food for the soul,*' So, now feed your soul with the peace and beauty in this garden, just as you feed your body with its fruits. It gives your soul peace and harmony. Son, may this peace be with you always. I'm leaving you with a gift, Jesus said. A gift from him whose story is the greatest ever told and told in the greatest book ever written—the Holy Bible. Find out why he called it a gift, and why he died trying to give it to you. It's all in here. This is for you."

"Never heard these things before," Dan said, staring at the Bible. "Who is wise enough to number the stars. They do not know where to find wisdom but death and destruction knows something about it," he murmured. "Destruction knows something about it," he repeated. "Is this the *something* I felt lifting the rocks?" He looked at the garden and heard the silence spoke to his soul one more time. "Yes! It was *the something!*" he asserted. "Food for the soul. From now on that's gonna be my breakfast, lunch, dinner and snacks in between."

Before Dan could say thank you, Brother Simeon was gone.

*   *   *   *

Now, indeed, Dan feeds his soul every opportunity he had. He would visualize the fine and perfect radiance of the sun that shoots through the leaves and feels this peace as if he were outside of himself. He would feel like the seed that just pops out of a dark womb, bursting with life. The walls around him do not seem to exist anymore. He feels bounded by nothing. He feels a new freedom. He becomes a new man.

"What happened to you, man?" Buster asked when he noticed Dan smiling. "What'ya got there."

"A bible," Dan answered.

"Ya understand that stuff, man?" Buster said. "My folks yacked about God all the time. I went to church with 'em when I was little but got pinched every time I got restless. Came in one ear and out the other, ya know."

"I do," Dan agreed.

"Is that why you smilin', man?" Buster asked.

"No," Dan said quietly, being careful not to offend him. "I'm smiling because I feel great. I got the Spirit."

"Da what?" Buster asked, incredulously.

"The Spirit—you know," Dan answered.

"What spirit ya talkin' about, man," Buster asked. Dan wasn't sure if he was curious or just being sarcastic.

"Spirit from the garden," he answered.

"Da what?" Buster asked again, incredulously.

"The Spirit from the garden," Dan said. "Go out there and smell the flowers. Get the feeling. Then you'll know what I mean."

"You nuts or somethin,' man?" Buster said, now giggling. "Me? Smellin' flowers, man? Na-ah. I ain't gonna smell no flowers. Na-ah. They'd think I'm crazy"

Dan laughed. "Let 'em think that way," he said. "Why should you care about what people think? You're not doing anything bad."

"Guess not," Buster said, "but smellin' flowers, man? That's sissy stuff, ya know." Dan laughed again. He could just imagine how Buster would look out there. His huge torso bent down, his large hands gingerly handling a delicate petal and sniffing it as he, self-consciously, threw glances around to see if someone would be watching him.

Buster was the leader of a gang of black inmates called the Busters. He got fifteen years for drug dealing, attempted murder and illegal possession of firearms. He was the muscle, the enforcer, like Dan's one-time sidekick, Muscle. He had already done eight years and would be due for parole in two. He did five years at hard labor. After that, he got assigned to the rec room. He also cleaned the hallways and other areas. He earned his new job by helping keep his fellow black inmates in line. Now and then he could even make requests to go outside—meaning inside the walls—in the garden.

Chapter 4

Dan hit the Bible. He took notes diligently like he did in poker. He wanted to learn more about the Spirit. At the very start, in the Genesis, he already sensed it. As he read on, he began to see a thread weaving through. He thought this thread is the Holy Spirit. If man had it, he would be rewarded. If he didn't, he would get punished. He saw human saga as a struggle between good and evil.

Man fumbled in the dark in search of the Spirit. He offered gifts and sacrifices to try to please and win favor from God. He prayed. He made rules of do's and don't, rituals and customs. He came up with laws. He listened or did not listen to men with visions, dreams and prophecies. He made a covenant with God and even used a big rock placed under a tree as the witness. Yet, he fell short.

Then along came Jesus, the Son of God. He came as a human being who also had feelings. He was logical, sincere and honest and spoke the everlasting truth. He would be called the Messiah, the Prince of Peace, *the* Christ. He would be the personification of the Spirit who would win over the evil. He would come up with the New Covenant based on the Spirit.

Dan now believes that the Spirit in a person is basically a feeling. It would be what Jesus and Psalms called the *Comforter* that gives intuition and instinct. It gives inner strength. It would be, as Brother Simeon said, the personal basis of his faith.

Dan felt the urge to share his new-found understanding. One evening, he tried to share it with Buster.

"I gotta tell you about Jesus and the Holy Spirit, man." Dan said.

"Hey, knock off the bullshit, man! I wanna go to sleep—ya hear me?" Buster growled. Dan's message promptly bounced off the wall. He knocked off his preaching for the day.

For days, Dan and Buster didn't say much to each other. One day, Buster just opened up. A gleamer cracked through the wall. It was like a seed breaking out. He'd been out in the yard a few times.

"I understand what you've been trying to tell me," Buster said. "I got the feeling."

*   *   *   *

Now, Dan and Buster studied the bible together.

"Listen to this," Dan said. "'*The little boy Jesus loved God so much and when he grew up he lived out his life in the lonely wilderness until he began his public ministry.*' This means that Jesus love for God means love for the silence and beauty in the wilderness, and through which he then came to understand God. This, in turn, means that if we have the same thing, we would understand God also, hence understand Jesus. Does this make sense?"

"Yes, it does," Buster answered in rapt attention.

"Here's another passage," Dan said, turning to another page: '*Jesus saw the spirit of God coming down in the form of a dove while being baptized by John the Baptist. He was baptized with water but Jesus will baptize you with the Spirit.*' This means that his baptism with the water was just a rite of passage to this spiritual experience. As Jesus was baptized symbolically with water by John the Baptist, so he would baptize others with the Holy Spirit, meaning the same silence or inner peace that comes from a dove or, for that matter, from Nature. It follows, then, that in order for anyone to get baptized by Jesus, he must also take the first step that Jesus took and that is, to find this inner peace in him in the wilderness. Therefore, baptism in this case is not just a ritual but an actual experience of this inner peace or Spirit.

"Yeah," Buster agreed.

"Now, listen to this," Dan said, turning a page. "'*That is what I meant when I said that no one can come to me unless the Father attracts them to me. Don't you believe that I am in the Father and that the Father is in me? The words I say are not my own but are from my Father who lives in me. But when the Father sends the Comforter instead of me—and by the Comforter I mean the Holy Spirit—he will teach you much, as well as remind you of everything I myself have told you. It is the source of all Truth. I am leaving you with a gift—a peace of mind and heart and the peace I give isn't fragile like the peace the world gives.*' Now, then, how can we say that the Holy Spirit, deep silence and inner peace mean the same thing in our discussion? I believe the answer is in here, in the 23rd Psalms, where it says: '*He leadeth me by the still water. He comforteth me.*' This is the same *Comforter* Jesus talked about in the previous passage. The 'He' here refers to Jesus. In the Book of Luke, he said: 'When I was with you before, don't you remember my telling you that *everything* written about me by Moses and the prophets and in the *Psalms* must all come true?' So Jesus leads us by the still water. This, then, is Jesus way of *comforting* us–or, for our discussion, baptizing or introducing us to the Holy Spirit."

"Makes a lot of sense to me," Buster said. "Jesus leads the way. We follow."

Dan came up with an idea to show his understanding better. "I'll put them together this way, so we can see even better," Dan said, as he put their experiences and Jesus' statements side-by-side, like a pair of x-rays placed side by side for comparison.

1) Both of us got attracted to the garden. (*The Father attracts them.*)

2) Then we saw the garden's perfect beauty and felt its serenity. (*The Father sends the Comforter—and by the comforter I mean the Holy Spirit.*)

3) The beauty and serenity told us something in a manner that is clear, simple and honest, giving us a certain perspective on everything we've heard and read about Jesus and God. (*He will teach you much as well as remind you of everything I myself have told you.*)

4) The garden pointed us the way to relate to Jesus. (*No one can come to me unless the Father attracts them to me.*)

5) It gave us peace of mind and heart. (*I am leaving you with a gift—a peace of mind and heart.*)

6) Our spiritual experience from the garden gave us an understanding that seems to be the truth. (*It is the source of all Truth.*)

"What do you think of that?" Dan asked Buster.

"Why, everything fits just perfect, man!" Buster said. "By the way, who told you all these?"

"Brother Simeon, a visiting preacher," Dan said. "Now let me ask you, do you now believe Jesus might've had the same feeling and that he nurtured it with this food for the soul?"

"Yes, indeed," Buster said.

"Let's continue," Dan said. "Furthermore, Jesus said: '*Those the Father speaks to, who learn the truth from him, will be attracted to me. Not that anyone actually sees the Father, for only I have seen him.*'" "For only I have seen him…," Dan repeated. "Can you believe that? And it says here: '*We know these things are true by believing not by seeing.*'"

"Believing? Yes! Right on!" Buster cheered and slapped hands with Dan.

"You know something?" Dan asked. "I don't think these things were ever told from the pulpit or anywhere else. They don't tell us that we shouldn't worship icons or statues or, at least, tell us that they are not the real source. They don't tell us that to get the real stuff, we have to go to Mother Nature."

"I don't think it'll ever happen, though," Buster answered. "Who would tell them? Not by the government. Separation between the church and state, ya know. But say what you have to say, I'd say."

"I believe so," Dan said. "This connection between Jesus and Nature has to be told. It is so important. I'll spread the word. You wanna join me?"

"Who—me? I don't know. I Could scare 'em into believing, alright," Buster replied. They laughed.

"*I believe and therefore I speak*," Dan said.

* * * *

Dan intended to speak out. He wanted the world to know. The Internet would come in handily. He started planning.

In college, Dan took courses in semantics and mathematics. He learned that thought processes work their way up or down to desired or useful levels of abstraction. In semantics, he learned that the "the test of abstractions is not whether they are higher level or low level abstractions, but whether they are referable to lower levels." Because the source of the spiritual feeling is nature—trees, flowers and the bees, and so on—it would be the lowest level of the abstraction ladder, or the foundation. He'd start from it and build things up, logically. He knew that if he went the other way, the way others do, he would he'd be vague and even emotional, just like speaking in tongues. He wanted to avoid being called a "windbag." He would speak from the heart, being the place where the Spirit lies.

Chapter 5

Dan appeared before the Parole Board as scheduled. They looked over his record carefully. They were impressed. They interrogated him about his plan for the future. He answered that he had a plan and that whatever else he would do, it would be a positive contribution to the community.

"Would you please tell us your plan?" a judged asked.

"I am thinking of spreading my understanding on the Lord Jesus, sir," he said in a soft, sincere voice, as he looked at the judges straight in the eye one by one. "I have this spiritual feeling. I have found inner peace and strength. It pulled me through in the worst of times. It would pull me through any time, anywhere."

The judges were impressed. Without further questioning, the Board approved Dan's release. They congratulated him and wished him success. They would send a copy of their decision to the job-placement section. Buster congratulated him, too.

Earlier, in anticipation of Dan's release, Buster called his dad to come and pick him up. When it was time for Dan to go, they embraced each other.

"Stay in touch, ya hear? Buster said, his voice cracking.

"I will, brother," Dan answered. "See ya out there soon."

* * * *

The heavy, steel gate clanked shut behind Dan. Like the rush of air he pulled in deeply, a feeling of freedom surged in him—the freedom given him back by society and the freedom his new self had given him. He looked at the trees as he walked briskly to a waiting car. A letter by Apostle Paul to the Ephesians came to his mind: "*He will give you the inner strengthening of His Holy Spirit…May your roots go down, deep into the soil of God's marvelous love…and may you be able to feel and understand, as all God's children should…Now your attitudes and thoughts must all be constantly changing for the better. Yes, you must be new and different person, holy and good. Clothe yourself with this new nature.*" Feel and understand, he repeated.

"Hi, Mr. Johnson! Thanks for coming by," Dan said, as he slid in and threw a plastic bag of belongings in the back and pulled the door shut. He held out his sun-baked hand to shake Mr. Johnson's hand. He is Buster's dad.

"No problem," Mr. Johnson said, feeling Dan's rough hand and strong grip in his frail hand. He took a glance at Dan. His beard and long hair half-covered his deeply tanned face.

"Just call me Willie. Ya look great, Dan!" Willie said.

"Thanks. I worked hard on it," Dan said, laughing. Willie laughed, too. "It's great to be out. Rough in there but I learned a lot."

"Buster told me that, too. Now he talked a lot about this spirit thing. He wasn't called Buster for nothing, ya know. Now he's a softy. I'm just too happy for him and you both. He also told me you and him gonna do the gospel. God bless you both. By the way, d'ya have a place to stay? Ya could stay with us, ya know."

"I got one lined up already. I appreciate the offer, though," Dan answered.

"How about some spendin' money?" Willie asked.

I'll be okay, thanks, Willie" Dan said, then turned silent. He was touched by the kindness of the old man, who reminded him of his dad. Memories came back to him. He said: "My dad left me some money. I got a check with me. He passed on a while ago. I Didn't even get to see him. I was knocked out from exhaustion at the time."

"I'm very sorry to hear that," Willie said and patted Dan's hand. "So where are we going?" he asked.

"Truth or Consequence street in Las Vegas. There's a bank there.

They stopped at the bank to cash Dan's check. It took him an extra time to do it because the bank had to check all his papers, including his new driver's license. They stopped by the Nursery to pick up the keys to his apartment and car. The car was bought by the nursery owner to be paid back from Dan's wages. He also paid three months advance rent for his apartment. The owner wasn't in at the time, but Dan talked to an employee who also wanted to see his papers before he handed him the keys.

Dan asked Willie to a hamburger, but said he'd had a big breakfast earlier. He offered to pay for the gas but Willie refused that, too. They embraced each other to say good-bye.

"Son, just call me if there's anything I could help you with—okay?" Willie said.

"Yes, I will and thank you, sir," Dan answered.

*   *   *   *

Dan watered the plants, helped customers load their buys, and kept the place neat and tidy. He loved it. It was a life on the beach for him, considering his prison life. He loved being close to the plants. In their beauty and perfection, he saw God's grand design. He saw the truth directly, simply and honestly. *"Now your attitudes and thoughts must all be constantly changing for the better. Yes, you must be new and different person, holy and good and clothe himself with this new nature,"* he recalled again. Yes, attuning his thoughts and feelings to them became

Dan's second nature. Even just a touch of a plant with his fingers would make him feel as if he were a part of it and all. He went through his job purposefully and quietly. He was very helpful and courteous to the customers.

Mark, the owner, was observing Dan. When he was getting ready to go home, Mark went to him and asked: "How did it go, Dan?"

"Oh, I just love it—thanks," Dan said, grinning. He took Mark's proffered hand and shook it.

"See ya tomorrow—take care," Mark said.

*   *   *   *

Dan's apartment was a small studio unit and sparsely furnished. But he loved it. He loved it, not in the same sense as the fancy condo, but for its simplicity. He wondered where to keep the couple thousand dollars he inherited. He put it under his mattress.

As he lay in bed, he wondered how he could best spread the Word: Bring the folks and kids to the nursery on Sundays? No. Mark wouldn't go for that. Go to the parks? Why not? Go to the schools? No, that's public property. They would call it proselytizing. Visit the homeless? What would I tell them to smell in the morning? Do miracle tricks? No, I wouldn't do that. Go to the strip and bark out like a street corner evangelist? He thought about the men and women passing out porno stuff and there, among them, calling out this God thing? He felt silly. Wrong place for the wrong reason? No, he reasoned. It would be the right place for the right reason, silly as it might seem. He thought he would give it a try.

Dan sincerely, if not passionately, wanted to share his understanding. Despite the odds, he felt he could win his case through reason. But what kind of reason would he need to have? He remembered a famous logician who said there is nothing wrong with religion itself, but that religions are bad for the most part. That is, bad from his point of view, maybe because he couldn't apply logic. And bad, for the most part, because of the way some religions are practiced today. Dan believed they are practiced, not for the Spirit as he understood it, but for political and economic reasons and for tradition's sake, that is, religion has become too ritualized. His thoughts turned to the religious wars of history, which Dan believed were waged for the same reasons. He thought he'd use the reason that comes from the heart: Love.

So, out of Love, Dan stood among the smut peddlers who lined the sidewalk where a stream of tourists strolled along one balmy Sunday afternoon.

"Hear ye! Hear ye! Listen and feel the silence of the green sky! Listen and feel the silence of the blue plants! Listen and feel! Hear ye!" Dan cried over and over.

They heard him, alright. They looked up the sky but did not see green. It was blue. And the grass was not blue. It was green. He got them talking and laughing. "This man must've lost his marbles"…"Hang onto your wallets"…"What's he—nuts?" A woman passing by heard him, too, but didn't look up. His voice sounded familiar, she thought, then stopped. She looked at him.

"Dan! Is this you? I can't believe this!" she exclaimed.

"Hello, Betty! You didn't even look up. You could've missed me. Good to see you, Betty!" Dan said, as he put out his hand to shake hers.

"Look up to what—to a poker lie?" Betty said, laughing. "Good to see you, too. Rather an unusual place to preach in, isn't it?"

"Yeah, like preaching at the Sea of Galilee, isn't it?" Dan said, laughing. "Wrong place, I imagine. I couldn't get their attention enough. Why, you didn't even look up!" He couldn't recall her ever looking up at the day or night sky while in their cruises.

"Are you really into this preaching thing?" Betty asked. "The pen sure'd changed you, didn't it. Listen, I'd like to hear more about this 'feel the silence thing' but I gotta run. Oh! Give me your phone." Dan gave it to her. Betty turned around then melted in the crowd. Dan caught a glance of her beautiful legs. He remembered the evening he last saw her. That was the straw that broke the camel's back. It hurt his feelings so bad. He compared his thoughts of that evening with the blue sky. He felt detached and peaceful. Now he even felt detached when he saw Betty's legs.

"Hear ye! Hear ye! Listen and feel the silence of the blue sky! Listen and feel the silence of the green plants! Listen and feel!" Dan cried over and over again. But he was ignored. "*They look but don't see, they hear but don't understand,*" he thought, recalling what Jesus said. But Dan was not discouraged. He knew someday they would look and see, hear and understand.

The tourists just ignored him—as they did with the peddlers, who made little clicking sounds with their wares before they stuck them out. There's a reason for that. They couldn't make contact with the passersby, a mistake Dan made when, as he pointed at the sky, he accidentally touched one who happened to be a plainclothes man. Dan got ticketed. He appeared before the Judge who dismissed the case with a warning.

He tried the park one beautiful spring morning. He approached a little girl who was looking at the bees and a tree full of blossoms.

"Beautiful, isn't it?" Dan said.

"Yeah," said the little girl.

"You know why they do that?" Dan asked.

"I donno," the little girl answered.

"They love each other," Dan said. A woman, who Dan presumed was her mom, heard what he said and promptly threw a fit.

"Get away from him, honey!" she barked. She whipped out her cell phone and called 9-1-1. It wasn't an emergency situation, but the woman got so frightened by the bearded, long-haired man. Dan didn't leave. He decided to stay. He went to talk to her to calm her down but she became even more frightened. A patrol car arrived.

"What seems to be the problem?" the cop asked the woman.

"He's molesting my daughter!" the mother said, angrily. "He's telling her he loves her. He's sick!"

"Did you tell the girl you love her?" the cop asked Dan.

No sir, I did not," Dan answered. "I was only telling her the relationship between a bee and a flower, one that's based on love, as God meant it."

The cop saw that Dan was sincere. He saw he made sense. He let him off but warned him to stay away next time. Dan understood the officer's reason. They both knew what's going on. Dan recalled what Jesus had said about this: *"But if any of you causes one of these little ones who trust in me to lose faith, it would be better for you to have a rock tied to your neck and be thrown into the sea."* He wondered: "What if a child loses, not only her faith, but her life too? Would Jesus get so mad, he'd throw us all into the sea like a barrel of rotten apples?" When he arrived home, he found the door jimmied. He looked for his money. It was gone.

* * * *

Dan was not discouraged. He wrote to the Department of Public Schools suggesting that, as an addition to a play area, a garden be built where kids could enjoy and take a moment of silence. It fell on deaf ears. He wrote to the State Department of Public Parks, who wrote back that public parks are just that—public, and that the Park's policy is not to endorse any particular religious viewpoint or orientation. He received the same response from the White House (through the U.S. Park and Wildlife Service). He suggested the same thing to the churches of various denominations, noting that the Spirit of God and Jesus could only come from God's handiwork, not from any human source including the bible. On this one, he received a sarcastic response from a preacher.

"Dear Dan," he wrote. "What do you mean the Spirit does not come from the Bible? As far as the Spirit goes, I must tell you that what nature could give, the Bible also could. To suggest that the Spirit of the Lord could not come from the Bible, because you consider it a human source, is a balderdash and just shows your ignorance of the Scriptures. They are our only source of the Word of God. It says from the start: "*In the beginning was a word and the word was with God and word was God.*" Moreover, Apostle Paul said in the Ephesians: '*If you say that you belong to Christ Jesus, and though you are far away from God, you have been brought very near to him because of what Jesus Christ has done for you with his blood.*' Does nature tell you what He did for you with his blood? Could you have known about this truth if you did not read the Book? So, then, the Bible could also be a source of the Spirit, is it not? I could tell you a whole lot more, but I let you find it out yourself. Read your Bible!

Your friend, in Jesus' Name,

Justin

* * * *

Dan took part in public meetings by the county and city councils. They appreciated his novel idea of a park with private area where a person could reflect undisturbed. But he was told that there are already plenty of parks around, where anyone could do this sort of thing if he wants to. There wasn't a peep from the crowd. But it caught the attention of a reporter. The next day an article about Dan appeared in the local paper. It was also distributed by wire across the country.

George read the article in a Seattle newspaper. It reminded him of a similar project that was started by a Seattle couple, where kids from the inner city and elsewhere could spend a weekend and learn about the environment. He thought of giving them a call but changed his mind. He wasn't sure if they would want to connect a natural thing to a "religious" thing.

George called the reporter who wrote the story to see if he could get hold of Dan. The reporter traced him to where he worked.

* * * *

"Dan? Hi! This is George, the dot-com guy from Seattle. Remember?" George said, catching Dan during his break.

"Well—hello, George! How've you been, pal?" Dan exclaimed.

"Just fine, Dan. How about another round of heads-up, huh?" George asked, jokingly.

Dan laughed. "I've stayed away from all that since you busted me. I'm into something new now."

"Yeah, I'd read about it. I like it. These days, I kind-a feel there's more to this life. Would you tell me about it?"

"Why, certainly," Dan said, "You see, I don't recall anything that was ever said about the link between man, nature and Jesus. Poets write about nature and spirituality but I don't think anyone has made the connection between the three. What I want to do is write and talk about this spiritual link."

"I haven't either. It sure sounds like a fresh idea," George said, "not that I listen closely to this stuff. So what's the Spirit and how does the connection work?"

"First of all," Dan said, "Jesus saw and felt this Spirit written in all of God's creation. Let's just say that what he read was God's own signature. He saw beauty, peace, reason, purposefulness, consistency, love, mercy and so on. Let's just say these are the big characters or the properties of this signature. And the small characters are the physical things—the trees, flowers, stars and so on. We see, touch, smell and feel them, and it is from them or through them that we can directly experience these properties. Jesus brought this Spirit into his heart and pursued its meaning, or as the Bible says *'God has put this knowledge in the heart.'* In the book of Luke, it says, *'As a little boy, he greatly loved God and when he grew up he lived out in the lonely wilderness until he began his public ministry to Israel.'* The Bible also says: *'Jesus saw the spirit of God coming down in the form of a dove'* while being baptized.' I take this to mean that the dove is symbolic of his right of passage to this spiritual experience, which is what John the Baptist meant when he said, '*I baptize you with water but he will baptize you with the Holy Spirit,*' meaning the Spirit that is found in Nature.

"This, then, is my goal: To spread the word about this Spirit—what it is, where it comes from and what it means to be called a Christian. For Apostle Paul had said: '*You can't understand the spirit unless you have it. And you can't be called a Christian unless you have the same Spirit Jesus had.*' The Spirit *in* us is also the key to understanding the Christian Bible, ourselves and our world.

"Jesus also mentioned '*food for the soul.*' Just as the fruits of a tree are foods for our body, the Spirit is a food for our soul, which is our heart and mind. Without this food for our soul, we would be weak *morally* because we would be weak in *will* and *determination,* just as we would be weak physically without physical food. So you can imagine how important this Spirit is. But it is tragic because, I believe, this thing is so misunderstood that instead of looking at a tree for its spiritual values, we would rather look at lifeless and meaningless icons or statues.

"Okay, I call," George said in poker lingo. "So, what's your plan, Dan?"

"Well, at this point, it seems like I'm not getting anywhere at all," Dan said with a sigh.

"To start with, I'd like to get some land where I could plant things and build pergolas where people could sit quietly and reflect. I'll guide them on how to attune their thoughts and emotions to the silence around them. This makes them aware of themselves. It has a cleansing effect in their souls. This is a start."

"I'm sold," George said. "Where do you want it?"

"I prefer it here in Nevada. Maybe in Las Vegas. My reason is the weather. Sitting in the shade would be more enjoyable. Besides, where else could you get a 'Sin City' for student?" Dan said, laughing.

"Yeah, like the poker players, huh? But you know what, Dan? I could've just given you back your money right then if you had told me about this," George said.

"I wish," Dan said, wistfully, "so I wouldn't have ended up in the pen to suffer. Good Lord! But that's where I learned this thing, though. But it doesn't have to be that way. I could've learned it with pleasure by this thing I'm talking about."

"Good enough. Let's get going," George said. "Just get the site and give me a figure. I'll be there to cut the ribbon—okay pal?"

"You got it. Thanks ever so much, George!" Dan said, excitedly.

Dan broke the news to Mark, who was taken aback. He didn't know Dan was into this thing.

"That's really great! We could supply all the trees and stuff," Mark said in jest, unsure if Dan was really serious.

But it gave Dan an idea. "I could do it here. Do you own all this spread?" Dan asked, sweeping his hand at the adjoining vacant land.

"Yes, all five acres. Is that enough?" Mark asked, again in jest.

"Two'll do," Dan answered, matter-of-factly.

"You got it," Mark said, now realizing this is what the prison job-placement meant by 'spirituality'. "You, as my next door neighbor, would add to my business," he said.

"I like the location, too," Dan retorted, "close to yours for added attraction." They laughed and shook hands. Mark told Dan he had friends who are builders and landscapers.

When Dan was done for the day, he called George and told him he found the land. He told him the price. He said he'd call again to let him know the cost of the entire package. George told him to have the owner sign an agreement of sale, put the deal in escrow and set it up as a Charitable Trust.

* * * *

George paid cash for everything at closing: land and improvements including a three-bedroom cottage with three baths and a parking garage for three cars, landscaping, appliances, furniture, computers and TVs. He also put up the fund for his expenses for one year. He also paid for his health premiums for the year. They did not expect any income except from donations, which they knew wouldn't be much, if any. But George would support him and some others if needed. He eschewed the idea of making a good living out of the project. Jokingly, he said he needed some tax shelter, anyway. But he loved "his" project and was very committed to it. He also told him if he needed anything else to let him know.

Chapter 6

George was also in his twenties when he became a multi-millionaire. He and Dan both got lucky. *They were at the right place and time.* But Dan's luck changed and ended up in a disaster. George luck ran out, too, but he knew when to quit.

There was also something that bedeviled both these men. In Dan, it was greed. In George, it was guilt. It was guilt over the death of Bobby, his kid brother. The memory remained fresh. It haunted him.

George was five years old and Bobby was four when a tragedy took place one summer day. They were outside in their backyard tossing a plastic ball to each other. When George threw the ball to Bobby, a puff of wind carried it away over the fence to the water. He told Bobby he was going to get their dad. He ran into the house and called him. Phil, their dad, wasn't there. He ran outside and found him in the front yard, looking over the roses.

"Dad, our ball went over the fence to the pond," George said.

"We'll fetch it," Phil said. George followed his dad. When they got there, the first thing they noticed was Bobby wasn't around.

"Where's Bobby?" Phil asked. The unlocked gate and the ball in the middle of the pond alarmed him. He began to worry. "Bobby, where are you! Bobby!" he called out, as he picked his way along the edge of the pond outside their neighbors' backyards. Getting no answer, he decided to go into the water. The wind had stopped blowing by now. He followed a straight line from the middle of their yard to the ball. As he waded out into the murky water at waist-deep, his foot bumped into something soft. "Oh, my God!" he gasped and dived in. He brought Bobby out of the water in his arms. Bobby's body was limp. His head, arms and legs dangled. Phil hurried to shore, laid him down on the grass and started to revive him. He told George to get the phone outside. He put his mouth on Bobby's and rhythmically pushed air into it. Phil got no response. George came running with the phone, dragging the long cord behind him. His dad dialed 9-1-1 and told him to tell what happened when the operator answered.

"No, my brother isn't breathing," little George said. "Dad, she wants to know our address." Phil grabbed the phone and rushed off the address and went back to Bobby. He dangled him by the legs and tapped his back. Some water came out but still there was no response. He did everything he could think of but none worked. The paramedics arrived and took over. They placed an oxygen mask over Bobby's face who, by now, had turned ashen. They took him to the hospital.

As they took Bobby away, George started to cry. "Is Bobby dead, dad? I'm very sorry, dad. It's all my fault! I shouldn't have thrown the ball to him!" he sobbed. His dad held him tightly. "Bobby will be just fine, son," he said reassuringly. But Bobby didn't make it.

So now there was just the two of them left. George's mom died soon after Bobby was born. During his teen years, George became the only survivor when his dad also passed away. An uncle of his took him into his home. He also provided for his school expenses He finished high school then left for college on a scholarship. He majored in Computer Engineering and graduated with honors, then found a job in a computer software company. He worked there for several years then, after cashing in a sizable stock option, started his own company. It prospered beyond his imagination. Years later, he sold it for a fabulous sum. This, plus his investments in real estate and stocks, made him a very wealthy man.

George lives by the lake. He has a yacht moored by. He travels in his private jet around the world for business and fun. He reaches out to the world around him and away from him through the various charities he had created in the name of Bobby, his dad, an uncle and others. Yet, in spite all these, the deep-seated guilt feeling has not left him. It is a festering sore. He saw several psychiatrists but to no avail. He and Diane go to church regularly but the rituals, sermons and social get-together just could not rid of it. He reads the bible. He loves the snippets of proverbs and sayings clothed in beautiful prose. But, for the most part, they are like *straws in the wind*. He needed something that would go down deep in him and uproots it. What Dan told him could be this something.

Chapter 7

The construction was completed in the spring. Dan put an ad in the local newspaper inviting the public to join him celebrate the opening of "WHERE TRUE PEACE LIES, a garden retreat where a unique, age-old concept of Spiritual Living will be taught. Location: Truth or Consequence Roads." He also sent invitations to several political dignitaries and the press. He informed friends. He wanted Brother Simeon to give the blessing. He called the penitentiary but was told that there was no such person there. Dan wondered whether he used a different name, but wondered why he would do that. Was he someone else? Dan was puzzled.

* * * *

George arrived in Las Vegas aboard his private jet the night before. He arrived at the occasion in a limousine. The small crowd gathered in the front yard. A sign over the entrance reads: WHERE TRUE PEACE LIES.

It would be a simple ceremony. To start, a Deacon from a nearby chapel gave the blessing. He wished Dan and his staff success. Then Dan took over.

"Thank you all for coming," Dan said, as he looked over the small crowd. "Thank you, George, for were it not for your wholehearted support, we wouldn't be here today. Thank you, Mayor...Congressman. I also want to thank our senator, who couldn't make it here with us, for his support and well-wishes. Thank you, Mark, for your help.

"You notice our sign Where True Peace Lies. That's what we hope to accomplish here: To explain what it means and find it. We didn't plan this project as a traditional place of worship. You notice there are no walls or roof. But it would be home to the Spirit just the same, the Spirit upon which Jesus had built his true church. We'll explain what we mean by this. We hope it would be understood not only by our heads but, more importantly, by our hearts.

"Now, I'd like to introduce to you my three good friends." Looking and pointing at them one by one, he said: "This is Buster, who loves to garden; Betty, our sandwich and home-maker. They did a superb job getting this affair ready on very short notice. And over there, our most generous benefactor, George. Thank you very much, George."

Eyes turned and lingered on Buster for his impressively large, muscular physique, but they lingered longer on Betty for her beauty, beautiful blue eyes and a lovely smile. The crowd clapped their hands.

Dan turned the mic to the mayor and asked if he would like to say something.

"Thank, you," the Mayor said. "I'm very happy to be here with you, here in this lovely place. Outsiders call our city 'Sin City.' Basically, it's a tourist town where millions come to visit and enjoy. But I see hypocrisy on their part when they call us that name, but would come just the same—even to live here. What we suggest they should do is drop this hypocrisy and just enjoy—enjoy the fruits of freedom they find here, as in the rest of our country. What we all must do, instead, is to learn to control ourselves. We cannot live from one extreme to the other. But with self-control we can live in moderation, the middle way, as Aristotle once said. We should do it where or when temptation begins to get the best of us, here in Las Vegas or anywhere else. This, rather than name-calling, would be a measure of our maturity as individuals and as a nation. I have a feeling that this new home of the Spirit, as Dan said, would teach us that.

"Gentlemen, I'm flattered. I'm proud that you have chosen Las Vegas as your venue. We want you. Our nation wants you. The world wants you. Go out and spread the Word. God bless and good luck"

The congressman took over the mic and said: "The mayor has said it all…and well. I'll help pass on the word. Congratulations to you Dan, Buster, Betty…George for your worthwhile endeavor. Good luck."

With soft drinks and sandwiches in hand, the visitors toured the place. Dan led them into the house, through the living room and into the kitchen and eating area. All the rooms and the kitchen opened to the outside scenery. As they stepped outside, Dan pointed to a restroom in a corner.

It was a beautiful spring morning, bright with a gentle breeze. All the fruit trees, roses and perennials had started blooming.

"What's this, Dan? A garden of Eden?" the Mayor asked.

"Actually, just a small copy," Dan said, half-jokingly. They followed the paved path that branched out to the six, two-sided, 7x7 pergolas or booths built close the block wall on the west side and facing the garden. They stepped inside them. The latticed panels and roofs were made of cedar 2x6s. Eventually, they would be covered by the honeysuckle vines that were planted next to them. Each room was furnished with a lounge chair, a side table and a comment box with note pad and pencil. In the north side, there was a tilled spot for vegetables. In the middle was a shallow pool where tropical fish would be planted. Water was fed from an underground source and regulated by an ultra-quiet pump. The source would serve all their water needs. Nearby was a water basin for the birds. Nesting areas were built in the corners, tucked in and protected so predators could not get to them. There were bird feeders, too.

A row of juniper lined the east wall. It would serve as a screen against future neighbors. Also, Dan wanted them there so that guests could observe the fine, silent radiance the rising sun makes through the leaves. Except for the pump, there was only the sound of nature.

"I already feel it," George said.

"Good," Dan said. "That's the seed of the Spirit. That's the first thing that must happen, just like it happened to young Jesus. As I said earlier, this happened to him when he was *lured by the Holy Spirit into the wilderness when he was a small boy. He loved God so much he spent a lot of time there before he began his ministry.* In other words, he went to the wilderness because he loved the peace and beauty, the birds and the trees, the flowers and the bees and so on. So then, he also had the seed of the Spirit. So then, as the Bible says, *in order to understand the Spirit, one must have the Spirit first. Those who have the Holy Spirit in them can understand what the Holy Spirit means then use the Holy Spirit words to explain the Holy Spirit facts. And in order for one to be called a Christian, he must have the same Spirit Jesus had.'* So then, we must have this seed in us before we can even begin talking about the Spirit or God or Jesus himself."

"Hmmm. Makes a lot of sense," the congressman, who heard it, said.

"Amen," said Willie. Dan nodded at him, approvingly.

When the open house was over, Dan gave out cards containing their mail and e-mail addresses and a telephone number. When all the guests had left, a reporter interviewed Dan and George.

"Hi, I'm Ted from The Nevada Clarion. I like this place, and your idea of a unique, age-old concept of spiritual living. Would you explain?"

"My pleasure," Dan said. "This concept is unique because, as I understand, there is only one man that I am aware of who came up with an understanding of the Spirit as the link between him, nature and the Creator. This man is Jesus, of course. He might have picked up a cue from the philosophers before him, the Greek Stoics who, in the 4th century BC, 'chose spots of great beauty in which to build shrines to the healing gods. These were described as places where the whole of the universe of men and nature come together in a single quiet order to be healed.' They also said that 'the greatest good, which is happiness, can be achieved by following reason, freeing one's self from passions, and concentrating only in things he can control; that each man has within himself reason which relates him to all other men and to the Reason (God) that governs the universe; that Natural Law was above civil law and that it provides the standard by which men's laws may be judged.' So, I say that the Spirit and Reason together made Jesus who he was. I mean, not only did he relate to his fellowman by Reason, he also related to them through this Spirit. He measured up to these standards.

"To understand the Spirit is to understand Jesus. It is also the key to understanding your self and your world. It is the key that unlocks the truly endowed self in you, the image of God in you, if you will. Jesus had promised this, being the Spirit himself and God's ambassador for it. But today, as in generations past, the source of the Spirit is misunderstood. Today, as then, man's sources remain the same—the idols and statues of whatever make and form. These, according to him, wouldn't help you understand him or his message. They would only lead to false understanding.

"To these spots of great beauty Jesus went or, again, as the Bible describes it, '*Then Jesus was led to the wilderness by the Holy Spirit.*' He became as *one* with it or, as he said, '*I am in the Father and the Father is in me.*' Likewise, it is our goal here: To connect ourselves to Nature, Jesus and God and become as *one* with them in spirit. How?" He pointed to his heart and said, "Through here."

"Another thing: I don't think the twelve apostles talked or wrote about the source of the Spirit in these down-to-earth terms. I think the closest one who came to it was Apostle Paul when he said: "*A secret had been kept for centuries and generations past. And this is the secret: that Christ in your hearts is your only hope of glory for God's secret plan, now at last made known, is Christ himself. In him lies hidden all the mighty, untapped treasures of wisdom and knowledge. When you came to Christ he set you free from your evil desires, not by a bodily operation of circumcision but by spiritual operation, the baptism of your souls. For in baptism you see how your old, evil nature died with him and was buried with him."* Here the baptism Paul referred to as the *'baptism of your souls'* was also the one John the Baptist referred to when he said. *'I will baptize you with water, but he will baptize you with the Holy Spirit.'* What John the Baptist meant was that Jesus would baptize you with the Spirit by leading you to the beauty and peace of nature. *'He leadeth me by the still water. He comforteth me,'* the Psalms says. The 'He' referred to here would turn out to be Jesus himself. For the *Comforter* mentioned in the Psalm is the same *Comforter* Jesus referred to when he said: *'The Father sends the Comforter instead of me—and by the Comforter I mean the Holy Spirit—he will teach you much, as well as remind you of everything I myself have told you. It is the source of all truths.'*

"So, this is where we come in: to get you in touch with nature and baptize or plant in you the seed or the Spirit of peace.

"So, then, it is obvious this concept is unique in a sense that the Spirit comes from only one source, that is from nature. It's not from the bible or from any written work as commonly believed or from any other human source. They call the bible the 'Word of God' but, really, it's just that—word. I mean, a "word" stands for something and this something could be anything to anybody. Unless we know the object that the "word" represents, we could get confused about it. I think this is one reason why Jesus said the Spirit does not come from any human source, and a reason why Paul called it a hidden secret. The bible was written, printed and bound into a book by man. It is like a recipe book that gives instructions on how to cook something but it's not the food itself. If you haven't eaten the food yet, you don't really know exactly how it tastes like. Therefore, the food is not the same as the instruction given in the recipe. As a Semanticist would say, the map is not the territory. Let's not get confused between the recipe and the food or the map and the territory. The taste is in the pudding; that is, go out there and watch and feel the changing color of the clouds as the sun sets, or watch the subtle motion as they pass by a tree. Jesus went to the wilderness to get this feeling. He communed with nature, the territory, the actual source of the Spirit.

"The bible talks about or refers to the Spirit in simple, eloquent and elegant prose, but it doesn't give you the real *feel* of the Spirit. It is a great literary art but it could get tricky to the unwary. Let me give you an example. Let's go back to the statement: '*As a boy, he was led by the Holy Spirit into the wilderness. He loved God so much he spent a lot of time there...*' Note the phrase 'was led.' It is passive, as if something was leading young Jesus, like a cow being led by the nose. Actually, he went out there on his own choice to feed his soul with the alphabet soup of the Spirit. He went out there to inhale the fresh air, to absorb into his heart the silence and beauty of his surroundings. He hungered for it, and hunger is something that could not be seen but only felt. So is the Spirit. It does not lend itself to imageries like a statue that is worshipped. And the worshippers get misled. Nature does not mislead. Its words are clear, simple and direct. It's as 'honest as day.'

"There's a lot to be said on how to free your self from your passion, how to understand yourself and the bible and so on. But what I'll just say here is the bottom line: the *feel* of this place which, again, is the *seed* of the Spirit from which our understanding and future discussions will grow. So, let's just say that the *feel* is the *seed* we'll be sowing here."

"I understand," Ted said, "can I call you the Thirteenth Apostle?"

"No," Dan replied, humbly. "I neither walked nor broke bread nor shared wine with the Man. Call me, perhaps, the Thirteenth Man because I share the same feeling the apostles had. I'll do what the Apostles did—spread the word about the Spirit but with an added meaning."

"What's that?" he asked.

"Nature, of course," Dan answered.

Ted turned to George. "And you put up the funds to build this place, right? I understand you're a multi-millionaire. What made you do it?"

"My kid brother. He...he died when he was only four," he said, hesitatingly. "I tell you, this thing touched me like nothing else ever did. Really, it's something no money could buy. It's well worth it to me."

"Thank you and wish you luck—both of you," Ted said.

* * * *

George told Dan, Betty and Buster that he would love to stay a while longer but he had to go home shortly. He had to be home for Diane who was in the hospital for cancer treatment. He made a quick dash to Las Vegas just for the inaugural.

He wanted to know more about his new friends. Earlier on, Dan told George a bit about Buster and Betty. He told him that Buster shared the same cell with him; that he was a violent man, but he is now such a gentle giant. The spirituality had given him tremendous self-control. As for Betty, he said she had broken up with him after he lost all his money. She married Pete, another poker player, but later divorced him after he also went broke. She married again and got divorced again. She has no children. She joined them because she sincerely wanted to turn her life around. Besides, she said, she had nowhere else to go to and nobody else to turn to. She lost her mom and dad in an auto accident many years ago.

* * * *

Before he headed for home, George took his friends to a dinner at the Bellagio, where he had already made reservation.

Buster couldn't believe it. There he was, in a limousine, sharing a ride with a very kind and rich man who took him as more than a friend. It was like a dream. His mind flashed back to his life in prison—to the letters he and Dan sent to the judges, who held the balance and set him free. He felt a deep gratitude.

George was sitting across him. He was very much impressed by this big and muscular man. He could just feel the fear he instilled in his enemies.

"Mr. George, I want to thank you and Dan for batting for me," he said, holding down his emotion. "That was the greatest thing that ever happened to me." Dan was sitting next to him. He put his arm around his broad shoulders.

"It's okay," he said, reassuringly. "And you have a yard job now besides, right brother?" Dan said, smiling. They laughed.

George turned his attention to Betty, who was seated next to him. He had seen her in the games Dan and he played together. But theirs was just a nodding acquaintance. He turned to look into her charming blue eyes.

"Happy chance, us coming together this way, ain't it, Betty?" George said.

"Yes. A very happy one, indeed," Betty answered, with that certain smile. "I was going through the roughest time of my life—no job, just divorced and stuff. I was walking along the Strip when I ran into this man. He was yellin' to the crowd 'Look and feel the silence of the green sky!' I paused and thought for a second. 'What? Green sky? Has this guy lost his marbles?' His voice sounded familiar. I turned to look. He has shoulder length hair and beard. And I said: 'Dan is this you?' So we chatted a bit then left. I said to myself: 'silence…peace…why, that's what I need.' Then I read about him in the paper. I called and told him I wanted to join him. He took me in. Now I'm their housekeeper and cook," she said, laughing. Dan, Buster and George were laughing, too. "Happy, indeed, how things turned out to be. The Lord's way, I guess."

"Yes, indeed. Here we are," George said, as the limo pulled up the valet driveway. The driver got out to open the door for Betty.

As they were walking through the casino, George asked, "Remember that day, Dan?"

"Yep. Who would forget it," Dan said. "And you know what? Now and then I wondered why you wanted to change the game to No-Limit."

"Oh, I planned it that way," George said. "I figured I could beat you only once and bust you. Sorry, brutal but it worked. I pulled this trick on somebody. I caught this guy with a better draw, though." Again George felt guilty and it bothered him.

"Good evening," a maitre d' greeted them. "This way please." He led them into the chandeliered room. Eyebrows went up. Except for George, the three were in casuals, which made them self-conscious. George noticed it.

"It's OK folks," he said. The host helped Betty into her seat, to a table meticulously dressed up in snow-white linen, artistically folded napkins, a fresh bouquet of flowers and shining silverware and crystal glasses.

"Mmmm-mm! What we got here. Never occurred to me I don't know how to eat." Buster said, amused and puzzled by the array of silverware. Heads turned and eyebrows went up one more time. He thought about his life in jail: the plastic spoons, forks and knives; the bare metal tables and the roomful of inmates in grays, seated to metal trays filled with slop. Now he was about to indulge himself in a sumptuous meal. One extreme to another, he thought. He knew he is neither one. Now, he has something special.

They took their time enjoying the meal, after all George made his own flight schedule—and he told them so. Buster savored the whole kit and caboodle that included a fair-sized sirloin steak grilled rare.

When they finished, they proceeded to the airport. George called his pilot, informing him he was on the way.

George brought up the question as to why Dan would consider Jesus as the only authority on their particular brand of Spirituality.

"What about those in the other religions, like Buddhism, Mohammedanism, Taoism and Shintoism?" he asked.

"Well," Dan said, "I have to admit I don't know much about the others. What I know came from gleaning the encyclopedia and dictionary. Buddhism teaches self-denial, Moslems did away with idols and consider Mohammed their prophet, Taoism, which also derived from nature, teaches simplicity and selflessness, and Shinto, Japan's state religion, 'emphasizes upon the worship of nature, ancestors, ancient heroes and—prior to 1945—the divinity of the emperor.' Prior to that time, the direction of Shinto, as espoused by the emperor, apparently was not love and peace. We say that our own Bible doesn't tell much about this nature link, so we presume their Books don't, either Therefore, Jesus is the only authority as regards to this particular spiritual view. Sorry, this is begging the question.

"From this particular spiritual viewpoint, we are also looking at Natural or Universal Laws. They are a uniquely simple and universal language, a physicist might say. All of God's creations communicate to one another in all kinds of ways (like men), however they all obey the same Laws. And they all do things for a noble reason and purpose, (unlike men sometimes, sorry to say). Our Bible says God created Man in his own image and breathed into him the life of the Spirit, just as it did to the rest of creation. But we blew ours with Adam and Eve, and won't be restored unless or until we are willing to learn and change. So *we know all these things to be true,* as Apostle Paul said. The question now is, are we going to believe and follow Him as he leads us by the *still water* to become *the image of God?* This is the crux of the New Covenant, by the way. My own understanding is that the other religions do not have a Jesus, a New Covenant and an 'image-of-God' thing to strive for. So, in this sense, I believe Jesus is the only authority. I hope I have given you a good answer."

"Indeed, you have Dan. Thank you," George said.

They arrived at the airport where George's gleaming blue aircraft was waiting. A uniformed pilot and a stewardess stood by the ladder waiting.

"I want you, folks, to meet them," George said. Dan, Buster and Betty got out of the limo to meet Rick and Paula.

"Well, folks, it's been nice seeing you all. Just let me know if there's anything else you need," George said and hugged each of them goodbye.

"Please give Diane our regards. All of us will be praying for her," Betty said.

The plane revved up and started to roll away. In seconds, it was up in the air. It turned around and when it came overhead Dan, Buster and Betty, it dipped its left wing to reveal a bold white logo on the tail fin that read WHERE TRUE PEACE LIES. They waved their hands. They felt proud.

"Hmmm-mm," Buster hummed and said, "Ain't that something? What a good man."

"And handsome, too," Betty rejoined, smiling. Dan heard it. They filed into the limousine and went home.

Dan's cell phone rang. "Did you guys see the logo? George asked. "I have it put in a couple of days ago. It'll help spread the news, don't you think?"

"Yes, it would," Dan answered.

Chapter 8

When they got home, Dan, Buster and Betty gathered around the kitchen table for a little talk. The hurried preparations didn't give them much time for it.

"So, how d'ya like this place?" Dan asked, looking at Buster then Betty.

"Real God-send," Buster said. "Thanks so much to you and George. I worked on a job the prison placed me on but I got laid off. I tried to get a job in the casinos and other places but they look at my history record and...ya know. I can't just loaf around, big and strong as I am. I was getting into my folks' hair. I should've gotten hold of you right after I got out and perhaps got a job at the nursery, too, but—anyway when dad got your invitation I thought I better run down here. You guys saved me." There was a moment of silence. Dan looked at Betty.

"I felt the same way. This is also the place for me." She said. "After I've gone through two divorces, I got so hopeless. I drank and hung out in the casinos. You know what I mean? But I've learned my lesson and I'll continue to learn."

"What happened to Pete?" Dan asked.

"Oh, he got busted. He left town—to find a new life elsewhere," Betty answered.

"So we're all here to make a new life—that with the Spirit," Dan said, "a life in which we are our best and happiest, regardless of our past or what we have or don't have." Just then the phone rang.

"Excuse me," Dan said, as he picked up the phone. "This is Dan."

"Dan, this is Michelle. I was there at your opening. I like the place. I have some questions for you. I'm gonna e-mail it."

"Sure—go ahead," Dan said. He hanged up and went back to the discussion, which turned even more serious. He opened his Bible and read a passage: *Whoever heard of someone lighting a lamp and then covering it up to keep from shining? No, lamps are mounted in the open where they can be seen. This illustrates the fact that someday everything in (men's hearts) shall be brought to light and made plain to all.* He explained: "What this passage tells us is that, first of all, we must look at ourselves honestly, like we're looking at ourselves in a mirror. This mirror is like the winking star upon which an innocent little girl asked: 'What is that I see? Is the star winking at me?' The star answered her as honestly as can be, and the child saw this honesty because she herself has an honest heart. The light is the Spirit of the star and the little girl. We look upon this light as a standard of honesty to measure ourselves up to. Let's compare our thoughts and feelings to this standard and ask, 'How honest am I?' There couldn't be a better mirror or standard than this. Do I make sense?"

"I'm not sure," Betty said.

"Sort of," Buster said.

"Think about it." Dan said. He decided to drop the subject for the time being. He thought Buster and Betty needed some time for the idea to sink in. They went outside.

"Buster, do you think you can handle everything around here—turning the soil, pruning, weeding, planting and all?" Dan asked.

"No problem. What a beautiful day! Hmmm-mm," Buster said then sucked in the air deeply, as he gently touched the dainty blooms of an apricot tree. "Ya know," he said, "I took over the garden when you left. I did all that stuff and I enjoyed very much."

Betty wasn't listening. She didn't seem interested. She left them and settled down in one of the booths. Dan understood why she couldn't be interested. He knew she had spent a good deal of her life in the shade of the night. He knew she needed some time to adjust to the light of day. He recalled the smile on her face when she mentioned the word "handsome" about George.

Betty sat in the booth and stared outside. She tried to focus but stray thoughts and jumbled emotions kept barging in on her. She couldn't keep still. She gave up.

"To heck with it!" she murmured. "It's almost time to cook now anyway." Then her cell phone rang. It was a male friend who wanted to set a date to go out with her.

"Cooking" that evening was a sandwich of tuna and minced onions mixed in mayonnaise, soda pops, potato chips and ice cream. But Dan and Buster didn't mind it at all. As matter of fact, they loved it. They figured, if they could survive the slop in prison, they could survive Betty's.

"Hmmm-mm, where'd ya learn all this, Betty?" Buster asked. Betty, who is used to fancy frills, said: "At the Bellagio." They laughed.

Michelle's mail came in. It read:

I'll start with your sign, Where True Peace Lies.

1) What is this Peace?

2) How do you know it is the true one?

3) A) Where is it found? B) How?

4) What good does it do for you?

Dan answered her right away. It went:
My answer to:

1) It is the Peace that lies in the heart. The heart gets it comes from nature through an intimate one-to-one correspondence with each

other. This is what I call "communion" with nature. For example: Have you ever listened to and felt the silence of dawn?

Jesus referred to this peace and quiet as "food for your soul," just like a fruit you eat is food for your body.

2) To start with, let me just call this silence one of the characters or properties of God's signature in nature—the Spirit. Others are beauty, consistency, purposefulness, love, mercy and so on. We sense or read these characters directly from natural things. We call these things the small characters.

These characters of the Spirit are the things pursued by Jesus when he was a small boy. To quote the Bible: "*He was led into the wilderness by the Holy Spirit. He loved God so much he spent much time there before he began his ministry.*" The "Holy Spirit" and "God" are just general terms to refer to the peace, beauty and others. (I'll tell you more about this general-specific relationship later on.) Wouldn't you consider the peace and quiet he found in the woods as true peace? I would. Where else could you find it? It couldn't come from a human source such as idols and statues carved from wood, stone, metal or whatever else.

3) A) The answer to this question is the same as in 2. I'll answer the B part: Just like you would taste a food with your tongue, you feel the silence with your heart. You stick your tongue out for the lick. But with your heart, you just sort of do the same thing until you feel it or, later, feel it as you visualize this source during a quiet moment. (At least, that's what I do.)

4) What can the Spirit do for you? The bible says: "*The heavens are made beautiful by the Spirit who gives intuition and instinct. It is not age that makes man wise. Rather it is the Spirit in man, the breath of the Almighty which makes him intelligent.*"

It makes you intelligent and wise. It gives you the foundation for a happier life. *Fear is nothing but the surrender of reason. In quietness is your strength.* So, this is what the Spirit of silence can do for you. Practice it.

I hope my answers are satisfactory.

Sincerely,

Dan

Dan saved Michelle's letter and his response. He e-mailed them to Betty, Buster, Ted and George. This would be his way of spreading the "Word."

*   *   *   *

They settled down to a routine. They continue to study the bible. Dan and Buster continue to be amazed by it. They discover a new thing everyday. Their attitudes and thoughts are constantly changing for the better every day.

They look around and see things that are not supposed to be. The people are worshiping the wrong gods, gods made of metals and stones against which Jesus had sternly warned them against. They think they are worshiping Him and they go home feeling smug. But these false gods don't help them change the contents of their hearts one bit, as Apostle Paul said.

They see the Spirit as a guide for man's individual conduct, just as they see the Stoics' Natural Law as a guide for Civil Law. They understand the reason why the Spirit is not spelled out in the U.S. Constitution, but they now know it is there, buried between the lines. They also know that the average citizen may not be aware of it or if he does, he thinks of it as a sort of Halloween ghost. They are squeamish about it. Hence, they insist that religion and government must not mix.

However, Dan believes the Spirit is not about religion (as he knows it). He thinks religion is too biased to see clearly that the Spirit is the essence of the individual, as it is the essence of nature, and that nature and natural law are above religion. So, again, there is this veil of misunderstanding that seems to cover the peoples' minds. So, again, if the great men of the world understood the Spirit in this manner, perhaps Jesus wouldn't have been killed.

"Oh, well," Dan said with a sigh. "We haven't matured enough. But we must continue to present the case of Jesus and his New Covenant. We must explain just what it is."

"Right on!" said Buster.

* * * *

While Buster and Dan are constantly changing for the better, Betty hasn't kept up. They were discussing something one day when she came out of her room all dressed up.

"I'll see you guys later," she said.

"Take care. See you later," Dan said.

"Ya sure look great, Betty. Hmmm-mm," Buster cooed.

Dan didn't ask where she was going or what time she'd be coming home. It wasn't that he didn't care. But here, in their household, they are free to come and go as they please.

* * * *

Dan was still up, reading the bible, when Betty walked in. She went past him, said goodnight (like an afterthought) and disappeared into her room.

The following morning, Betty fixed breakfast as usual, but she didn't join Dan and Buster at the table. She went outside to eat in the booth. Suddenly, she began to notice the little things around her: the gentle swaying of the slender apricot branches; the fine radiance of the rising sun through the leaves, the lovely flowers and so forth. She felt peace. The violence of last night came to her fresh, but she saw it now with a feeling of detachment. She saw the difference between the violence and the peace.

She saw Dan. As usual, he was eyeballing and feeling the plants.

"Good morning, Dan!' Betty called out.

"Mornin,' Betty,' Dan answered.

"Real nice out here," Betty said. "This place is like the lighted lamp thing you told us."

"What do you mean?" Dan asked.

"Well…" she said, hesitatingly. "I had a rough night last night."

"I'm very sorry to hear that," Dan said.

"I think I now understand what the lamp means. I saw the light—the difference when I start to notice the little things around here," Betty said.

"Difference? Difference from what?" Dan asked.

"What happened to me last night," Betty said. "I had sex with this man then he robbed me."

"Really? How awful!" Dan said.

"Yes," she said. "But these little things around here told me something very clearly, and gave me a clear choice," she said seriously.

"Good for you," Dan said. "Sometimes we learn this lesson the hard way, although we need not to. There's one man who didn't. He was an ascetic. He was also a great teacher and a leader or educator."

"What's that and who's that man?" Betty asked.

"It's a practice in rigorous self-denial," Dan answered. "Jesus did it. I don't think a lot of people know about this. But knowing this aspect of his life would help enlighten them as to who he was and why he did what he did."

"What did he do and why?" Betty asked.

"I give you an example," Dan said, quickly turning the pages to a passage and read: *Then Jesus was led out into the wilderness by the Holy Spirit, to be tempted by Satan. For forty days and nights he ate nothing and became very hungry. The Satan tempted him to get food by changing stones into loaves of bread. It said it would prove He is the Son of God. But 'No!' said Jesus. 'For the Scriptures tell us that bread won't feed men's soul.' Satan tempted Him again when it said it would give Him the nations of the world and all their glory if He will only kneel and worship it. But Jesus told Satan to go away, telling it that the scriptures told him to worship only the Lord God. He said He only obeyed him and that obedience to every word of God was what He needed.*

"You see, Jesus did not yield to the temptation by Satan. Why not? Because he was showing us, fellow humans, that resisting temptations is the solution to human folly. How? Through the Spirit.

"This is the same Spirit that Adam and Eve lost in the Garden of Eden. They lost it when they got tricked by the same Satan into believing they would become wise by eating the forbidden fruit of the Tree of Knowledge. But instead of becoming wise they became as fools and suffered like you and I.

"The Satan does its dirty tricks through our weak hearts and ignorant minds. But Jesus knew all about him and his bag of tricks. He knew the Scriptures well, and he was pure in Spirit.

"The Satan is really the evil in us. Jesus said: "*It is the thought-life that pollutes. For from within, out of men's hearts, come evil thoughts of lust, theft, murder, adultery, wickedness, deceit, pride, dishonesty and all other folly.* Winning the struggle against this evil in us, then, is the same thing as resisting temptations. He also said: "*I will explain mysteries hidden since the beginning of time.*" The solution to all our folly is one of these mysteries, and the search for the solution involves finding the *Good Heart,* for inside this heart you'll find just the opposite of the evil thoughts, which are love, mercy, peace beauty, honesty and so on. He found back the Spirit that was lost by Adam and Eve. So now he said: "*I am from A to Z, the beginning and the end.*" He was saying he was the Spirit since the beginning of time or since Adam and Eve. He was, is and will be.

"So how did Jesus find this Spirit? Note this statement: *Jesus was led out into the wilderness by the Holy Spirit.*' What do you think this means? It means he went out there to feed his soul with the alphabet soup of the Spirit—the peace and beauty in nature. He hungered more for them than Satan's offers of bread and possessions. So that, hungry and weakened as he was, he didn't even yield to the temptations. Satan sweetened his temptations but still Jesus didn't give in. Satan's trick worked with Adam and Eve but not with him. Why not? He had a disciplined heart and the iron will. The 'food for the soul' gave him this strength. At near death, he said: 'My body is weak but my spirit is willing…' That's how strong his will and determination were.

"With the Holy Spirit, you would have control over your emotions or your self. Without it, Satan would have control over them or you. So it did to Eve. So it did to you. You both yielded to temptations right? Interesting comparison, isn't it? Now you've found the Spirit. You've just been baptized with it. Now, nurture it like a little seed in you. If you pray for help, do it as Jesus said: '*When you pray, go away by yourself all alone and shut the door behind you and pray to your Father secretly, and your Father who knows your secret will reward you. It is not where you worship but how—is our worship spiritual and real? Do we have the Holy Spirit help? For God is the Spirit and we must have his help to worship as we should. The Father wants this kind of worship from us.*'

"This is another passage about this Spirit. Jesus said: '*You can't come to me unless the Father attracts you to me. When the Father sends the Comforter instead of me-and by the Comforter I mean the Holy Spirit—he will teach you much, as well as remind you of everything I myself have told you. It is the source of all truth. I am leaving you with a gift—a peace of mind and heart and the peace I give isn't fragile like the peace the world gives you. This not from a human source.*"

"The *Comforter, Holy Spirit* or the peace you felt are—for self-control purposes—the same. Feed your soul with it and get your strength from it. Come out here often. Let Jesus be your role model in discipline from now on. Measure up to him. Jesus was a wise man. We are fools. He is our way to salvation from our weak hearts and foolish minds. Congratulations. You made a momentous choice."

"Thanks, Dan," Betty said.

Dan left and went back into the house. Buster came out and saw Betty looking around the garden.

"Mornin,' Betty!" Buster said.

"Beautiful day!" Betty proclaimed. "I feel great! Oh, such a peaceful, wonderful feeling! Dan called it the Spirit."

"A love letter signed by God, huh, Betty? I'm very happy for you," Buster said and put his arms out. Betty put out hers, too, and they embraced. Some men in the nursery saw what they did.

Later that night, Buster was awakened by a flickering glow in his room. He heard popping noises. He peered through the window and saw a cross burning.

"What in the hell's goin'on here!" Buster exclaimed. He rushed out his room and rapped Dan's door. "Dan, wake up! There's a cross burning outside!"

They went outside to look. The glow of the fire lighted three white men standing by the road watching. They went out and approached the men.

"Did you folks do this?" Dan asked, unassumingly.

"Why should we—you phony ass!" one of them sneered.

"Betty—call the cops!" Dan called out. Betty was standing at the doorway.

"Yeah! Go ahead bitch! Ya nigger lover!" the other one yelled. He was a big guy. Instinctively, Buster made a quick one-two step towards him and threw a punched that sent him flying backwards. A melee quickly ensued. Buster punched another one and knocked him down, too. Seeing the power of the man, the third man got scared. He ran to his car and took off.

Three patrol cars arrived, each carrying two uniformed officers. They positioned their cars between the two groups. One of them asked questions from Betty then Dan and then Buster. Another one talked to the two men. They denied burning the cross. One said they were just passing by when they saw the fire and stopped to watch. He pointed at Buster and said he assaulted them. They said they would file charges. They signed a complaint. One of the officers called in for a background check on Dan and Buster. He found out they are both convicted felons and parolees. But, because of the assault, only Buster was handcuffed and taken to jail. Dan assured Buster that they would help him all they could.

Sometime later, Dan called George but first, he asked how Diane was doing.

"So these guys saw Buster and Betty hugging and got ticked off," George said.

"Probably," Dan said. "But the reason they were hugging was that Betty was joyous over an experience she had had earlier. She said she had never felt that way in her life."

"I see," George said.

"I'll call a lawyer first thing in the morning then go see Buster," Dan said. "I'll let you know," Dan said.

"Please do. Let me talk to Betty," George said.

"Hi, Betty. I'm sorry you guys got roughed up last night. How're you feeling?" George asked.

"A little shaken but I'm okay now," Betty said. "I couldn't believe these guys. A bunch of bigots!"

"That's ignorance and hatred for you," George said. "This odor is so bad it fowls the air. Just stay the course—don't worry." George assured her.

"Thank you ever so much and please give our regards and best wishes for Diane," Betty said.

"I will, and thank you," George said.

✻ ✻ ✻ ✻

"How you doin,' Bust?" Dan asked, hinting at humor. He talked by a phone from the other side of a glass panel that separated them

"Okay," Buster said, smiling faintly. He waved his hand at Betty.

"Hi," Betty said, waving back.

"I talked to George last night," Dan said. "He'll see you through this. I'll call him as soon as I've talked to an attorney. How about the lawyer you had—you wanna use him?"

"Yeah—he's alright. I'll give you his phone. You got a pen and paper?" Buster asked.

Dan pulled out a pen and a notebook from his pocket and wrote it down.

"Won't be long," Buster," Dan assured. "Thank God for George. This guy is all heart. I'll call Willie, too. Poor man, I sure hope he ain't worried."

"Oh, my folks are used to this old me," Buster said. "But dad ain't doin' too good these days. He had a stroke and wheel-chair bound. Mom does pretty much everythin' 'round the house. Who's gonna take care of the yard while I'm here?"

"Oh, don't worry. Betty will," Dan said. "You see, she could use a good workout. Right Betty?" Dan asked, turning his head to Betty and let out a chuckle.

"You see what—I'm not that fat!" Betty retorted. They laughed.

"See, we already miss you," Dan said. "We'll get you outa here real quick. George had already authorized me to sign a check for your bail. We're heading out to the lawyer from here. You take care, brother, okay?" Dan said as he spread his hand against the glass. Buster put his against it.

"Bye, Buster," Betty said and waved at him again.

"Bye, and thank you both and George so much. Say hello to Diane for me," Buster said.

Dan called the lawyer from his cell phone. The lawyer was in.

The lawyer had already started inquiring. The bail was set for $50,000. Dan wrote a check for the bail in the name of the Trust and gave it to him. He wrote another check for the retainer fee.

"I have a copy of the charges," the lawyer said. "We might run into some problem here unless we get a witness or evidence linking the cross-burning to those guys. And when we do, we'll throw the case back at them. We might need a private investigator. I'll let you know when."

The checks had to clear first and the release paper signed before Buster could be freed. Later on, that same day, the lawyer called Dan to inform him that Buster was ready to be picked up. Dan went to pick him up.

When they got home, Dan had an e-mail from Michelle. It said: "I read on the paper about what happened last night. I was in the nursery. I was looking for some plants when I noticed these guys looking at your place. I heard one of them said, 'tonight.'"

Dan responded right away. He asked Michelle if she would be able to recognize the men in a line up. He also gave her his phone number. Michelle called back right away. She believed she would recognize them.

Dan gave the information to the lawyer, who passed it on to the police who found out that all three men belonged to a white supremacy group. They were also convicted felons. A few days later, the police rounded them up. Through a one-way mirror, Michelle identified the trio as the men he saw in the nursery. They were arrested as suspects. Michelle testified at their trial. And so did Dan, Betty and Buster. On the strength of her testimony alone, all three men were convicted. Charges against Buster were dropped.

When the trial was over Dan, Betty and Buster thanked Michelle.

"That's the least I could do," Michelle said. "I believe in what you folks are doing."

"Thank you very much," Buster said and hugged her. He turned to look at the criminals. He caught hateful glares in their eyes.

"Damned fools. When will they ever learn? Hmmm-mm," Buster murmured.

Chapter 9

An e-mail came in from Ted. He asked : 1) How would you compare today's religious idols and rituals to those used by Israel during Jesus' time? 2) What, from your point of view, is baptism and communion? 3) What is the "Spirit?"

Dan's response:

I'll start with a statement made by Jesus: *"You must have no idols. Never worship carved images or obelisk or stone."* The dictionary describes *Idol* as: An image, phantom 1) Any image of god, used as an object or instrument of worship. 2) Any object of ardent or excessive devotion or admiration. 3) Anything that has no substance but can be seen as an image in a mirror 4) a) Any image or effigy b) an impostor 5) Logic—a material fallacy resulting from some common prejudice.

This is a working definition. It describes the idols used by the Pharisee (a member of a Jewish party or fellowship that carefully observed the written law but also accepted the oral, or traditional, law); and the Sadducee, (a member of an ancient ruling hierarchy, that accepted only the written law and rejected the oral, or traditional, law; and opposed to the Pharisee).

Now what do the churches of today have for symbols or idols? Wooden or stone figures of Jesus, Mary and the saints or some other revered figures.

To the use of these idols, Jesus made this scathing remark: *"What profit was there in worshiping all your man-made idols? What a foolish lie that they could help! What fools you were to trust what you yourselves had made.*

"Woe to those who command their lifeless wooden idols to arise and save them, who call out to the speechless stone to tell them what to do. Can images speak for God? They are overlaid with gold and silver, but there is no breath at all inside!

"But the Lord is in his holy Temple; let all the earth be silent before him, him who is Lord who created the seven stars and the constellation Orion, who turns darkness into morning, and day into night, who calls forth the water from the ocean and pours it out as rain upon the land. Seek him."

As regards to rituals, Apostle Paul had this to say about the Jews: *"When you came to Christ he set you free from your evil desires, not by a bodily operation of circumcision but a spiritual operation, the baptism of your souls. For in baptism you see how your old, evil nature died with him and was buried with him; and then you came up out of death with him into a new life because you trusted the word of the mighty God who raised Christ from the dead."*

Catholic baptism is also a ritual. I, myself, was "baptized" as a catholic when I was a baby. As I see it today, it involves the pouring of water over the head of a newborn child, as a priest solemnly declares: "I baptize you (name of the child) in the name of the Father and of the Holy Spirit..."

The act of communion is also a ritual. You walk up to the altar and receive the "body of Christ" with a wafer placed in your mouth and drink his "blood" with a sip of wine from a common glass. Worshippers think these are the real things. But Apostle Paul had this to say about them. *"They have no effects when it comes to conquering evil thoughts and desires,* the *spiritual operation in which your old, evil self was buried with him and come out of death with him into a new life."* So then what is the real communion and baptism? Before I give my answer, let me quote some statements from the Bible. They make some references to these rituals.

1) By John the Baptist: *"Someone is coming soon who is far greater than I am, so much greater that I am not even worthy to be his slave. I baptize you with water but he will baptize you with God's Holy Spirit!"*

2) From the Book of Matthew: *"Jesus was led into the wilderness by the Holy Spirit. He loved God so much he spent much time there before he began his ministry...Jesus saw the spirit in the form of a dove while being baptized."*

3) By Jesus: *"No one can come to me unless the Father attracts them to me. Don't you believe that I am in the Father and that the Father is in me? The words I say are not my own but are from my Father who lives in me. But when the Father sends the Comforter instead of me—and by the Comforter I mean the Holy Spirit—he will teach you much, as well as remind you of everything I myself have told you. It is the source of all Truth. I am leaving you with a gift—a peace of mind and heart and the peace I give isn't fragile like the peace the world gives you."*

Let me explain these statements by way of a couple of experiences I had in the "wilderness." I consider them my "baptism" and "communion." (By the way, I can understand general statements better when I relate them to specific things, such as my own experiences.)

On John the Baptist's statements: I was sitting outside in my backyard one calm and beautiful morning. I was out there to clear away mental cobwebs and to pacify my emotions when, all of sudden, right before my very eyes, I noticed a cluster of clouds moving by so subtly. I noticed it because of a leafy tree that stood between me and them. Without the tree, I'm sure I couldn't have noticed the subtle motion.

The gently gliding clouds made me feel relaxed and better thoughts came to me. It was like the Lighted Lamp thing. The tree and the passing cloud made it plain for me to see some thoughts that shouldn't be.

Now I look for this thing to clear my mind and calm me down, for instance when I'm stuck in heavy traffic. I call this my own baptism into the Spirit.

On the Matthew statements: My other experience was more personal and intimate. It made me feel as if I am out someplace where "all the earth is silent before Him," that is, I felt really connected to nature. I call it my communion. Once again, I was sitting outside before a tree, just looking at it when it just seemed to talk to me and said:

Come, Listen To Me

"Look at me carefully. Take your time. I am patient.
See me for what I really am, and you'll find that I more than what you think I am.
Notice and feel my stillness. Hear and feel my silence, and you'll do away the confusion in your mind and becalm your trouble heart, just as I clean the air you breathe.

I am in you and you are in me and the rest of the garden under the sun and the stars. I am, as you are, with the seasons. I am pure in spirit.

I give you flowers to enjoy in the spring and a shade for your summer respite. I give you colors in the fall. I give you beauty that is natural. I have the fortitude to withstand the winter storms, for my roots are anchored firmly in the soil, like my faith in my Creator. I give you Love and Life. That is my only purpose for being.

I stand here without judgment about you. Come and listen to me. Give me your thoughts and feelings and I'll give them back cleansed with the spirit of peace and love that's God's, that's in me."

So this is the baptism and communion I take. They are more real than the rituals. I suggest you do the same thing. Sit in front of a tree, or some such thing, and read my "Come Listen To Me." You'll know exactly what I mean. You'll feel what I felt.

On Jesus' statements: I relate my two experiences to them. I'll put them next to his statements, like comparing two x-ray pictures. This gives a better understanding.

1) By the stillness of the leafy tree, I *noticed* the subtle motion of the cloud. (*The Father attracts me...*)

2) Then my troubled thoughts cleared away and I felt peace at heart. (*The Father sends the Comforter—and by the comforter I mean the Holy Spirit.*)

3) This serenity taught me something in a manner that is clear, simple and honest, and gave me an understanding of Jesus and the Lord. (*He will teach you much as well as remind you of everything I myself have told you.*)

4) The cloud and the tree pointed me the way to relate with Jesus. (*You can't come to me unless the Father attracts you to me.*)

5) It gave me peace of mind and heart. (*I am leaving you with a gift—a peace of mind and heart.*)

6) My spiritual experience from Nature gave me an understanding that seems to be the truth. (*It is the source of all truth.*)

This comparison seems to tell me that Jesus was taking about my experience. Now, just like he had demanded from his listeners, either I say, "Yes, I believe" (that what I felt is the Spirit)" or "No, I won't." I say, "Yes, I believe."

The baptism that John the Baptist gave to Jesus was only symbolic. It was a rite of passage to his new life with the Spirit. So you see the difference between symbolic rituals and meaningful experiences. The real one is really spiritual. I believe Apostle Paul referred to this understanding when he said:

"*You cannot understand the spirit unless you have it. You cannot be called a Christian unless you have the spirit of Jesus Christ.*"

The cloud and the tree telling me what not to do and my instinct and intuition telling me what to do, is like Apostle Paul giving me this advice: "*I advise you to obey only the Holy Spirit's instructions. He will tell you where to go and what to do, and then you won't always be doing the wrong things your evil nature wants you to. For we naturally love to do evil things that are just the opposite from the things that the Holy Spirit tells us to do; and the good things we want to do when the Spirit has its way with us are just the opposite of your natural desires. These two forces within us are constantly fighting each other to win control over us, and our wishes are never free from their pressures.*

But when you follow your own wrong inclinations your lives will produce these evil results: impure thoughts, eagerness for lustful pleasure, idolatry, spiritism (that is, encouraging the activity of demons), hatred, fighting, jealousy and anger, constant effort to get the best for yourself, complaints and criticisms, the feeling that everyone else is wrong except those in your own little group—and there will be wrong doctrine, envy, murder, drunkenness, wild parties, and all that sort of thing. Let me tell you again as I have before, that anyone living that sort of life will not inherit the kingdom of God...

But when the Holy Spirit controls our lives he will produce this kind of fruit in us: love, joy, peace, patience, kindness, goodness, faithfulness, gentleness and self-control.

It is this God who has made you and me into faithful Christians and commissioned us apostles to preach the Good News. He has put this brand upon us—his mark of ownership-and given us his Holy Spirit in our hearts as a guarantee that we belong to him, and as the first installment of all that he is going to give us. Stop evaluating Christians by what the world thinks about them or by what they seem to be like on the outside. Once I mistakenly thought of Christ that way, merely as a human being like myself. How differently I feel now! When someone becomes a Christian he becomes a brand new person inside. He is not the same anymore. A new life has begun!

To understand the Spirit, you must have the Spirit in your heart. To be called a 'Christian' you must have the same Spirit Jesus had. We know these things are true by believing, and not by seeing."

My experience lent deeper meaning to the words of Jesus and Paul. That's how I can say "Yes, I believe." That's how I "know." Jesus said be logical. I think I am logical. I couldn't say this about my old experiences with idols and rituals.

Now you know what the Spirit "is" and where to find it. Now go get it.

Thanks for asking me these questions. I hope I've answered them to your satisfaction. I would be happy to answer more questions. Please be in touch and help me pass the word around.

Sincerely,

Dan

Dan framed copies of his "Come, Listen To Me" and hanged them in the booths. He also gave copies to Buster and Betty. He also e-mailed his response to George and Michelle. Dan followed up his e-mail to George with a post card for Diane, wishing her a speedy recovery. He, Buster and Betty signed it.

CHAPTER 10

▼

Dan wanted to further explore the truths about the Holy Spirit as the *"source of all truths,"* the truth that the *deepest thoughts of many hearts shall be revealed and the truth that is revealed in little children;* the truth that *we know these things are true by believing, and not seeing;* and the truth posed by the question: *"Who is wise enough to number the stars. They do not know where to find wisdom but death and destruction know something about it.* He also considered the truth about the miracle of Jesus rising from the dead and the other miracles he did (as mentioned in the Bible). He felt these are truths of God and about God. They are eternal truths. But, first of all, he asked: what is "truth"? He checked with the dictionary. He found three definitions that he liked: 1) sincerity; genuineness; honesty 2) The quality of being in accordance with experience, fact, or reality 3) agreement with a standard, rule, etc. that accord with fact or reality. To this definition, Dan added logic.

The definition and a question sent to him by Sam—a theology, math and science professor—gave Dan an idea. Sam also mentioned that he had read in the paper about his responses to other questions and he liked them. Dan was equally pleased to know that his message was starting to go around.

Sam's question was: How would you connect God, science and math/logic? What is the role of the mind and the heart in all this? How does Jesus come in? Could you explain the miracle of Jesus rising from the tomb?

Dan's reply:

Sam, I appreciate your taking the time to ask me these questions. I like them. I, myself, have been toying with similar questions for sometime. Now your questions and some standard (a definition) gave me an idea.

Okay, here I go. In college algebra, there is this concept called set—like a set of trees in a park, or a set of parks in a city, or a set of all the parks in the U.S. or even a set of all the planets in the universe. I call a set that contains all these natural things as its elements a *Natural* set. We see, feel, touch, hear and smell these things. It is also where the characters of God's signature or the Spirit (such as peace, beauty, love, mercy and so on) can be *perceived* and *felt* directly by the heart. Now I assume a larger, non-physical set containing, as its elements, all unexplainable events or phenomena like miracles. It also contains the *Natural* set as its subset. I call this set a *Supernatural* set.

Now, there is this thing I heard on TV about a certain behavior of sub-atomic particles called "quarks" which in their own "quarky" way would appear in two different places at the same time (a sort of double vision by the observer, perhaps). Our math teacher, who was studying for a Ph.D. in physics, told us that this phenomenon went against the accepted law of physics of "one-place, same-time" occurrence for all physical objects. A Nobel physicist described this in a more dramatic way: A dead cat is inside a bottle and a live one exactly like it (not a cloned one, mind you) is outside of it. The only problem, according to him, is that the dead cat is too big to be replicated quark by quark into a live one. A kind of "dead-and-alive" thing that appears inconsistent, isn't it?

What could this mean? Could it mean that any event that takes place on earth would have an exact counterpart (or mirror image, perhaps) somewhere else and vice-versa? Now I wonder whether some "miraculous" event that took place on earth—like the biblical account of Jesus rising from the dead and others—didn't also take place in the *Supernatural* set at the same time (like the "dead-and alive" cat). (By the way, the Bible says *"Everything on earth is a copy of heaven."*)

Further, assume a still larger set I call the *Superset* that contains, as its elements, the so-called Platonic "forms" or "ideals" (for example a perfect rectangle, square, justice, mathematical forms or numbers, etc. Plato might have named the Superset as the "One" which the Encyclopedia describes as "the real world where divine reason is like a light that shines through the darkness, like the Ideal Man in his book "Plato.") The *Supernatural* and *Natural* sets are its subsets.

Now, there is an article I read about a famous logician named Kurt Godel. He was a friend of Albert Einstein. Godel worked out the "exact solution to the heart of Einstein's general theory of relativity. His analysis reflects the distinctive characteristics of all his work. It is original and logically coherent, the argument set out simply but with complete and convincing authority." It went on to say that in 1931, when Godel was 25, he published his *"incompleteness theorems* that rewrites the ground rules of modern science much as Einstein's theory of relativity did 15 years before. He also demonstrated that "elementary arithmetic is incomplete and will remain so; and that whatever axiomatic system you base your calculations on, there are true statements that lie beyond the system's reach and that adding such statements to the system as further axioms will do no good. The enriched system is also incomplete, the infection moving upward by degrees." It described Godel as "a mathematical Platonist, who argued boldly that human intellect is capable of perceiving pure mathematical abstractions, just as human senses are capable of grasping material objects." So, up to this point, all the sets are "incomplete."

Lastly, I assume the grandest set of them all, an all-inclusive set I call the *"Domain of God"* that contains the other sets as its subsets. Herein lies the *Spirit*, the *Word*, or *God*. It is all in all. In other words, they are all one and the same. "*In the beginning was a Word and the Word was with God and the Word was God...God made things out of nothing.*"

As I mentioned earlier, the Spirit is God's signature in Nature. And among the characters in this signature are love, mercy and peace. While the mind perceives mathematical abstractions and Platonic ideals, the heart *feels* these characters. In other words, what the heart feels, the mind can't, obviously, for it cannot feel. So what the mind cannot understand, the heart does. The heart of Jesus understood. The bible refers to this kind of understanding: "*God had put this knowledge in the heart and the heart of the wise man is understood by wisdom. The spirit of wisdom is benevolent, and will not free evil speakers from his words. God is witness to his feelings and a true searcher of his heart and hearer of his tongue. He will be the greatest joy of many others. And the deepest thoughts of many hearts shall be revealed. In him lie hidden all the mighty, untapped treasures of wisdom and knowledge.*" All these words belong to the Domain of God or Heaven. Only Jesus had *seen* this Kingdom. He had both the heart and mind to understand. When he said, "*And the Last Day I will cause all such to rise from the dead,*" I believe him.

So it would be a sad day when Simeon prophesied: "*A sword shall pierce your soul, for this child shall be rejected by many in Israel, and this to their own undoing.*" It was also a sad day when Jesus said: "*Daughters of Jerusalem, don't weep for me, but for yourselves and your children. For if such things as these are done to me, the Living Tree, what will they do to you?*" A sad day for all, indeed.

Thank you for your letter, Sam. I hope I've answered your questions satisfactorily.

Sincerely,

Dan

* * * *

Sam sent another e-mail. He said: Your response to my first questions made a lot of sense. They are fairly consistent and logical. My question now is this: How would you bring this broad picture down to a more meaningful and useful level? For instance, you said that your main goal is to spread the 'Word' on how to win the struggle against the evil in us. You said, Jesus said: "*It is the thought-life that pollutes. For from within, out of men's hearts, come evil thoughts of lust, theft, murder, adultery, wickedness, deceit, pride, dishonesty and all other folly.* You also mentioned that the solution to all this folly is one of the mysteries hidden since the beginning of time. You believe that the solution involves finding the *Good Heart* for inside this heart you said you've found just the opposite of the evil thoughts which are love, mercy, peace, beauty, honesty and so on. I agree that these are great human values and are at the heart of who Jesus was all about. That, I could see. But I'd be a fool if I tell you that I could see how the Good Heart follows from your discussion of sets. So, would you show a connection? An example, perhaps?

Thanks again.

Sincerely,

Sam

Dan's reply:

Sam, first of all I want to thank you for your nice compliment. Before I proceed with your request, I'd like to say that, after all this time, I really haven't heard much talk about the Good Heart and how it is obtained. Or should I say, when people do talk about it, they are usually vague and meaningless. They leave me with more questions than answers, or leave me confused. I just don't understand them. Whether I believe them or not is another matter, however.

Okay, two things I'll do here: Give you a hint of the Good Heart and try to show you how it connects to the big set or the Domain of God the big set or domain. I'll do this by comparing an article and a letter from Diane. (By the way, she and her husband George funded our garden, Where True Peace Lies, and support our activities.)

I quote her letter:

"Dear Dan,

Thank you for sharing your thoughts with us. I have been going through a lot of pain, fear and anxiety just lately. But my "communion" and "baptism" with the tree did something so marvelous for me. It was only this morning that I could go outside with George. We have copies of *Come, Listen To Me* with us.

We sat side by side on the patio, facing the blooming trees and the lake. Beside us were these lovely pots of flowers. The sun was coming up from behind us, washing our garden and the lake with a delightfully cool, brilliance. Oh! What a magnificent morning!

Magnificent—yet impersonal! And seemingly indifferent as usual. But then as I silently read *Come, Listen To Me* and, at the same time, felt between my fingers the softness of the petals, something very unusual happened. There came a new awareness to me, as if a film suddenly peeled off my eyes and everything around me became more alive and personal. I felt as light as the light around me. I felt as if I was outside of my self. I was totally free! Free from fear, anxiety and my pain-wracked body! Oh! What a glorious a feeling! George told me that the peace he felt was so deep it reached down to the very root of his guilt feeling.

And you know what? I learned a lesson, too. The tree judged me not whether I am a Jew or a Gentile, a Protestant or a Catholic, a Buddhist or a Moslem, a black or white, a yellow or brown. It made no difference to the tree. It made no difference to God at all!

If death should come to me, may this freedom be with me forever, the freedom Jesus himself had.

Thanks to you ever so much and KEEP SPREADING THE WORD!

Sincerely,

Diane"

Sam, wouldn't you agree Diane's letter reveals a good heart? And a peaceful and tender one at that?

Now let's compare Diane's letter with the following article:

WHO IS THE TRUE GOD?

When you look at the sky on a clear night, are you not amazed to see so many stars? How do you account for their existence? And what about the living things on earth—colorful flowers, birds with their delightful songs. All of this could not have come about by chance. No wonder many agree with the Bible's opening words: "In the beginning God created the heavens and the earth"!—Genesis 1-1.

Mankind is greatly divided on the question of God. Some think that God is an impersonal force…But the Bible reveals that the true God is a real person who shows warm interest in us as individuals. That is why it encourages us to "seek God," saying: "He is not far off from each one of us."—Acts 17:27.

What does God looks like? A few of his servants have seen visions of his glorious presence. In these he has symbolized himself as seated on a throne, awesome brightness extending from him. However, those who beheld such visions never described a distinct face. (Daniel 7: 9, 10; Revelation 4:2, 3) That is because "God is a Spirit"; he does not have a physical body. (John 4:24) In fact, it is impossible to make an accurate physical image of our Creator, for "no man has seen God at any time." (John 1:18; Exodus 33:20) Yet, the Bible teaches us much about God.

Obviously, Diane's letter is so much more meaningful than this article. It doesn't even answer the question posed by the title. I don't mean to be overly critical but, in general, religious talks tend to be this way.

They tend to go round and round in a confused manner. They couldn't seem to go down to some meaningful level.

Now, how can I say that Diane's letter connects with the "Word" in the Domain-of-God set? The following, I hope, will show how.

In his book, *Language in Thought and Action*, Professor S. I. Hayakawa wrote: "The test of abstractions is not whether they are 'higher level' or 'low-level' abstractions, but whether they are referable to lower levels...If one makes a statement about 'culinary arts in America' one should be able to refer the statement down the abstraction ladder to particulars of American restaurants down to Mrs. Levin in the kitchen...A preacher or a politician whose high level abstractions can systematically and surely be referred to lower level abstractions is not only talking, he is saying something. As *Time* would say, 'No windbag, he.'

"The famous injunction of Jesus *'And as ye would that men should do to you, do ye also to them likewise,'* is, from this point of view, a brilliant generalization of more particular directives—generalization at so high a level of abstraction that it appears to be applicable to all cultures."

So Jesus injunction is an abstraction that belongs to the highest, all-inclusive set called the Domain of God. And the "more particular directives" the author might have referred to are the elements that belong to the lower set—those which the heart feels, such as love (even loving your enemy) and mercy, among others. They, in turn, might have come from even more particular directives, such as the natural love of a tree to share its fruits with the birds or humans and so on. The tree loves the birds and birds love the tree back—that sort of thing.

Solving a mathematical problem works the same way. In arithmetic, we add, subtract, multiply or divide until we arrive at an answer. Better yet, here's an algebraic example that illustrates this abstraction ladder better:

$$x + 4 = 5$$
$$x = 5 - 4$$
$$x = 1$$

Let's take another example. Take the words "Word" and "Name." If they do not refer to lower abstractions or particulars or are not used within proper contexts, they would not mean much to a listener, I don't think.

Diane's letter is different. It has meaning. She knew what she was talking about and the reader understands it. Her letter is built on facts. She used the *Spirit words to explain the Spirit facts,* so to speak.

Diane's feeling firmly rested upon this foundation. If you ask her if it gave her "faith," I'm sure she would say in a heartbeat, "Yes!" But without this foundation, what would someone mean if he says he has faith in the "Name" (of Jesus for example) or in the "Word" (of God)? He may mean anything or he's just guessing. He can't point to where his understanding came from, but rather quotes a passage, then quotes another quote to explain the previous quote and so on. So he floats like a balloon or a windbag. He can't come down and point to specifics upon which the "Name" was built, and he expects his listener to believe him. Hence, unless he touches base with Nature (as a particular directive), his understanding has no footing at all, or would be incomplete just as Godel's arithmetic (at the higher end) is incomplete. So, again, there's the veil that covers his heart and mind.

The Bible says: *"Even now when the Scripture is read it seems as though their hearts and minds are covered by a veil, because they cannot see and understand the real meaning of the Scriptures. Yes, even today when they read Mose's writings their hearts are blind and they think that obeying the Ten Commandments is the way to be saved. The veil of misunderstanding can be removed only by believing in Christ."*

How do we believe? "What is that I see? Is the star winking at me?" a little girl asked. "There came a new awareness to me, as if a film suddenly peeled off my eyes!" exclaimed Diane. Diane and the little girl are telling us how to remove the veil: feel like them. This is the way to understand the real meaning of the Scriptures and to become a Christian. That's the way to believe. The feeling is the mother of faith. Now what is faith? Faith (by definition), is a complete trust that my understanding of Jesus is true. "Know me," Jesus said. I believe I do. This faith is borne from the womb of my heart. From this womb to God—there's the connection.

*   *   *   *

Jesus gave this warning: "*We must use correct words and be logical, for by our words we shall be judged.*" He was logical, indeed, any way you look at his statements. "*I am the A and the Z…the beginning and the end.*"

So it is logical to say that the peace that Diane felt as she read *Come, Listen To Me* was what Jesus meant when he said: "*I am leaving you with a gift—a peace of mind and heart and the peace I give isn't fragile like the peace the world gives you.*" It is the same peace the Greek Stoics meant when they said the "whole of the universe of men and nature come together in a single quiet order to be healed." I say then that a heart at peace in this manner is a Good Heart.

All this reminds me of the letter I received from a minister a while back. I quote his letter:

"Dear Dan,

As far as the spirit goes, I must say that what nature could do for you, the Bible could, too. To suggest, like you did, that the Spirit of the Lord could not come from a human source—that is, the Holy Bible—only shows your ignorance with the Scriptures. The Scriptures are our only source of the word of God. It says from the start: '*In the beginning was a word and the word was with God and word was God.*"

Moreover, Apostle Paul said in the Ephesians: '*If you say that you belong to Christ Jesus, and though you are far away from God, you have been brought very near to him because of what Jesus Christ has done for you with his blood.*' Does Nature tell you this? Could you have known this truth if you did not open the Book? So the Bible is also a source of the truth, including the Spirit, is it not? I could tell you a whole lot more, but I let you find it out yourself. Read your bible…"

For a while I couldn't figure out what he meant by "Jesus Christ has done for you with his blood." The letter tells me that the minister sticks around on a certain level of abstraction. This is the same thing the other Minister (whose article I just quoted) did. I'd say both ministers got their cups upside down. No wonder their words are empty of meaning.

Perhaps I should add here that we (being lesser humans) couldn't always follow strict logic and use the correct words, like Jesus said. We could use our instinct and intuition which, according to the Bible, the Spirit gives. But, then again, King Solomon gave this advice: *"But though God has planted eternity in the hearts of men, even so, man cannot see the whole scope of God's work from beginning to end."* That is, all men except Jesus, for *"in him lie hidden all the mighty, untapped treasures of wisdom and knowledge."* Simply put, nobody–except Jesus-is perfect.

Jesus, the Great Teacher, said: *"The words I say are not my own but are from my Father who lives in me. When the Father sends the Comforter instead of me—and by the Comforter I mean the Holy Spirit—he will teach you much, as well as remind you of everything I myself have told you."*

The peaceful feeling Diane had was the *Comforter*. It came from Nature in no uncertain terms and filled her cup. Apostle Paul said: *"God had put his brand upon us—his mark of ownership—and given us his Holy Spirit in our hearts as guarantee that we belong to him, and as first installment of all that he is going to give us."*

If death should come to Diane, the Spirit would be a guarantee that freedom would be hers forever. Jesus, the Messiah, the Great Teacher has one student, Diane, with whom he did not die in vain.

This, I believe as true.

Sincerely,

Dan

Post Script (and a long one!):

So we are careless with our words. Jesus said something to this effect when he talked about the Pharisees who rejected God's plan for them and refused John's baptism. They are illogical. He said: *"With what shall I compare them? They are like a group of children who complain to their friends, 'You don't like it if we play wedding' and you don't like it if we play 'funeral!' For John the Baptist used to go without food and never took a drop of liquor all his life, and you said, 'He must be crazy!' But I eat my food and drink my wine, and you say, 'What a glutton Jesus is! And he drinks! And has the lowest sort of friends! But I am sure you can always justify your inconsistencies."*

Why—we do the same thing! So we pray, and if this doesn't work we justify ourselves and say, "It's God's will." One minute we say Jesus died for our sins, then the next minute what do we do? We go on in our sinful ways because we are "forgiven" anyway, or we don't care or just simply mindless and ignore him. The truth is, we are not "forgiven."

Listen to Apostle Paul. He told us what Jesus wanted us to do when he said: *"I advise you to obey only the Holy Spirit's instructions. He will tell you where to go and what to do, and then you won't always be doing the wrong things your evil nature wants you to. For we naturally love to do evil things that are just the opposite from the things that the Holy Spirit tells us to do; and the good things we want to do when the Spirit has its way with us are just the opposite of your natural desires. These two forces within us are constantly fighting each other to win control over us, and our wishes are never free from their pressures.*

But when you follow your own wrong inclinations your lives will produce these evil results: impure thoughts, eagerness for lustful pleasure, idolatry, spiritism (that is, encouraging the activity of demons), hatred, fighting, jealousy and anger, constant effort to get the best for yourself, complaints and criticisms, the feeling that everyone else is wrong except those in your own little group—and there will be wrong doctrine, envy, murder, drunkenness, wild parties, and all that sort of thing. Let me tell you again as I have before, that anyone living that sort of life will not inherit the kingdom of God...

But when the Holy Spirit controls our lives he will produce this kind of fruit in us: love, joy, peace, patience, kindness, goodness, faithfulness, gentleness and self-control.

Those who belong to Christ have nailed their natural evil desires to his cross and crucified them there.

If we are living now by the Holy Spirit's power, let us follow the Holy Spirit's leading in every part of our lives...

Don't be misled; remember that you can't ignore God and get away with it; a man will always reap just the kind of crop he sows! If he sows to please his own wrong desires, he will be planting seeds of evil and he will surely reap a harvest of spiritual decay and death; but if he plants the good things of the Spirit, he will reap the everlasting life which the Holy Spirit gives him.

What's more, *Apostle Peter said: "Come to Christ, who is the living Foundation of Rock which God builds. As the Scriptures express it, 'See, I am sending Christ to be the carefully chosen one, precious cornerstone of my church, and I will never disappoint those who trust him.'"*

"*Come to Christ,*" Peter said. But then Jesus said: "*You can't come to me unless the Father attracts you to me.*" Diane went to the tree and her communion with it gave her peace. This is the touch of Jesus, the *Spirit* or the *Rock*—the rock foundation upon which God built his church.

So, I'm not being misled when I say that we are not forgiven or automatically freed from the grip of our evil hearts when Jesus died, but, rather, he wanted us to change our evil nature through him or the spirit. He showed us how. He was a great Teacher, a role model who practiced what he taught. But do we understand or listen to him with our hearts? No. "*Great men of the world have not understood it. If they had had it they never would have crucified the Lord of Glory.*"

There's a proverb that went: "*He who knows not, and does not know that he knows not, is a fool, shun him. He who knows not, and knows that he knows not, is a child, teach him. He who knows, and knows that he knows, is wise, follow him."* This man is Jesus. He was logical. He did not go round the roses with high-in-the-sky words like a windbag.

So let's follow the advice of Apostle Paul and get rid of our emotional baggage and become as light as Diane with the Good Heart.

Thanks again. I enjoyed the conversation. Please pass the word around.

* * * *

From France came this e-mail from Claudette.

She said: If it's true that the so-called Big-Bang created the universe and man, then the biblical claim that Adam and Eve originated from a piece of clay is false. If so, then statements that follow from this premise are also false. The angels are an example. The Big Bang gives proof. Why aren't there proofs for angels? Now I'm even skeptical about prophesies, visions and dreams. They are like fairy tales.

Sincerely,

Claudette

Dan's reply:

Dear Claudette,

Thank you for your letter. You've raised a very good question.

Being based on physical evidence, the so-called Big Bang theory is *provable,* while the biblical account of the Creation is not—at least not with a test tube. What the bible writers have is a collection of historical facts and eyewitness accounts gathered from centuries of research. Certainly (?), if the writers had found evidence of the clay or an angel's remains, they would have presented it. But there is none. All they have is a truism, a faith and a linguistic metaphor *"From dust you came, to dust you shall return,"* and took it from there. There's a world-full of evidence on man's return to dust, however. But this fact and truism don't apply with the winged angels. So they accepted (or assume) the angels as not coming from dust but from "God." They live in heaven, Jesus said. They also accepted as "facts" the historical accounts of dreams, visions and prophesies, and eyewitnesses accounts of the miracle of Jesus' birth and his rising from the tomb. All these sound like fables, alright. For the truth in all this is not found in the test tubes of science but in its own logic that puts these fables, eyewitnesses accounts and other things into a consistent pattern that makes a lot of sense to me. This logic is the track I have wanted to follow.

What I'll do here is give you a bit of this logic, which I believe runs through the entire biblical saga.

To start with, the Book of Genesis tells us about God creating Adam and Eve, and putting them in the Garden of Eden. God's beautiful garden it was. And God's beautiful children they were, for they were pure and innocent. God created them in his own image.

But Adam and Eve would lose their good standing with God. This happened when they disobeyed God's warning not to eat the fruit from the Tree of Conscience or Knowledge, for its fruit would "open their eyes and make them aware of right and wrong, good and bad, and they would be doomed to die and return to dust from which they came." But a serpent (Satan) tricked them, convincing them that eating the fruit would enable them to distinguish between good and evil and that they wouldn't die. So Eve gave in to the temptation and ate the fruit then shared it with Adam. It opened their eyes alright. They suddenly became aware of their embarrassing nakedness.

So God drove them away from the Garden. As Eve's punishment, "she shall bear children in intense pain and suffering; yet even so, she shall welcome her husband's affection, and he shall be her master." For Adam, because "he listened to her wife and ate the fruit, God had placed a curse upon the soil, and all his life he will struggle to extract a living from it. All his life, he will sweat to master it, until his dying day."

Adam and Eve became ordinary mortals like us. Like us, they became aware of right and wrong, good and bad. And, like us, their minds and hearts were weak to counter the larceny Satan put into their hearts. This larceny is temptation.

Along came Jesus. He saw the problem. He declared: *It is the thought-life that pollutes. For from within, out of men's hearts, come evil thoughts of lust, theft, murder, adultery, wickedness, deceit, envy, lewdness, slander, pride, and all other folly"* He also saw the solution, and this solution involves finding the Spirit or the Good Heart. It would rid the larceny in men's hearts and strengthen their minds. And this Spirit would be found only in the same place where it was lost—the Garden.

A scientist can be a spiritual man and a spiritual man can be a scientist. But the logic of his science and spirituality take him into two different paths and these paths don't meet. If he mixed them, he could get very confused. I think this is one of the reasons why a line was drawn to separate the government from religion.

I hope you'll find my answers satisfactory. I'll e-mail you my discussion about the Spirit. It'll tell you my reasons for saying that the Spirit is beyond science. I'll also send you copies of a one-to-one talk with Nature (the communion) titled *Come, listen to me,* Diane's letter, and my answers to Michelle's and Sam's questions. My mail to Sam describes my understanding of Jesus rising from the dead.

Thank you very much for sharing your time with me. Would you pass the word around?

Sincerely,

Dan

* * * *

While Dan busied himself answering questions and spreading the *Word*, Betty and Buster did likewise in their own routines. They give an important support role to Dan. Without them, he'd have a hard time carrying on.

Besides her usual chores—laundry, cooking, cleaning—Betty now also raises chickens in coops she built near a corner. She secured the area with a wire fence. She loves to go out early in the morning with apron, sloggers, wide-rimmed hat, basket and a small knife. She collects the eggs. She boils, fries or makes omelet of them with the tomatoes, eggplants and scallions that she gathers. She cooks them the way "her boys" like them. She even has her own recipe book now, although she cooks fairly simple dishes. She even leads them in thankful prayers.

She helps with the yardwork, too. So does Dan. He helps Buster turn the hard soil and cut the grass. They lift weights together. They do it in one of the booths before the sun rises. Then they'd rest up before they hit breakfast. After that, they'd go back outside. They'd just sit in their own booths quietly as they soak in the silence and beauty around them. Dan particularly loves to watch the sun makes a halo of fine rays through the leaves. It helps him focus. He would close his eyes and visualizes the brilliant rays. He marvels in its perfection, beauty and deep silence. At the same time, it makes him aware of every little thought and feeling he has. The perfect silence and beauty of just this one piece of God's work give him a perfect guide to judge his thoughts and feelings by. It works like a laxative to his soul. It clears his mind and calms his heart before he sits down and does his work. Buster and Betty do the same in their own ways.

* * * *

At one time, Dan thought about panhandling, but he dropped it when he read that some folks were not being honest. Then luck came down to him as though from heaven. It came from George.

Now he sits in safety inside his home and, at the click of the mouse, sends out messages to his growing correspondents around the world. So Dan doesn't have to go around like the apostles did and who got mugged, robbed and jailed. But the cross burning came to them just the same. Dan understood all too well what lurks in men's hearts. But that's the more reason he continues on.

The modern computer does a miracle job. Dan thought that if the apostles had the same tool, their message would have been far better understood. Like the stick in a running relay, the same stick transfers from one runner to another unchanged. This couldn't be said of a message that travels by word-of-mouth over a long time and distance. By the time the King James Version of the Bible came out, Jesus and his Message had became "religionized". It had morphed into so many religions that Dan sees today. He thought the *Living Tree* had gotten all choked up by the moss and overgrowth of rituals. Dan hoped that, through the computer, he could strip them all off and let the sunlight in and lays bare the Message once more: that there is only one universal, rational and spiritual God; that this God is in Nature and that Nature alone is where the heart gets true understanding of this Message from.

* * * *

Richard, a philosophy student from New York asked the following questions: Why did Jesus call the Pharisees and Sadducees teachings 'yeast'? What did he mean by *"the source of all truth is not a human source?"* Why was Jesus called the *"Prince of Peace"*? What is Stoicism and how does it tie in with Him and the U.S. Constitution?

Dan's response:

> I'll start with the last question and proceed backwards: From the Encylopedia, I understand Stoicism as a way of life in which "The greatest good, which is happiness, can be achieved by following reason, freeing one's self from passions, and concentrating only in things he can control. That each man had within himself reason, which relates him to all other men and to the Reason (God) that governs the universe. That natural law is above civil law and that it provides the standard by which men's laws may be judged."
>
> Freedom is a bird in flight. That's a natural law. The U.S. Constitution, which is a set of principles, guarantees this freedom for all its citizens in their pursuit of "Life, Liberty and Happiness." However, in the pursuit of this happiness, a citizen sometimes forgets reason and self-control and disobeys the law.
>
> America is a land of milk and honey, someone said. An immigrant is not about to hold himself or watch his diet and say, "Look at all the fat and calories!" at the sight of a food-laden table. Rather, he'd help himself and he's happy and thankful. But he'd suffer consequences sooner or later. We all do, if we don't exercise moderation.
>
> Reason and self-control are assumed in the Constitution, and the idea of the Spirit is behind this assumption. It is there in a very quiet way—just as it does in Nature. There are reasons for burying it there (and keeping it buried), one of which is the fear that it could be misunderstood and the ghost of the Dark Ages could rear its ugly head one more time. It was an age when "writers accepted popular stories and rumors as true." It was an age of ignorance. I presume some of these stories that survive to this day are religious beliefs.
>
> We see traces of these beliefs today. They are misunderstandings about the Spirit. For example, if you walk into almost any church today you'll see icons and statues. Even so, they are tolerated. The

Constitution leaves them alone, but drew a line between the Church and the State, leaving the individual citizen to believe what he wants to.

But, in between the lines, the Spirit is there. Like Natural Laws by which men's laws may be judged, it is there by which the character of the Individual and the Nation may be judged. It is there to keep the Captain of the Ship of State in a steady course in calm or stormy seas. It is there as our *Rock Foundation*.

Extremely important, therefore, this Spirit isn't it? But, first, we must understand what it really is. Who is the authority on this? Jesus. "*I am the A and the Z, the beginning and the end,*" he said, referring to himself as the Spirit. Let's understand how he came to be and follow his example. This is how I came to understand the Spirit.

The Spirit is expressed in Natural (God) Laws that all of creation obeys. Jesus reflects this obedience. He said: "*Obedience to the words of God is what we need.*" And how did he obey? By freeing himself from his passions so that he could follow reason. For us to be able to do this, we also need the help of the Spirit. I get mine from nature (for instance, the radiance of the sun through the leaves). This helps me control my negative thoughts and emotions and makes me peaceful. *When the Holy Spirit controls our lives he will produce this kind of fruit in us: love, joy, peace, patience, kindness, goodness, faithfulness, gentleness and self-control.*" We need this to become better citizens.

We have just the opposite when the Holy Spirit is not controlling us. We even create our own god. We worship idols and statues made of wood or metal. There is not a breath of life in them, said Apostle Paul about these things. They work as opposite to the Spirit. What has breath of life in them? The small characters in the signature of God—the trees, the birds, the flowers and the bees—the source of all truths.

Throughout biblical history, God had subjected his chosen people—the Jews—to so many "trials and tribulations" for violating his laws. Time and again God—through his servants the prophets Moses, Simeon, John the Baptist and others—had forewarned them to turn themselves around from their "stubborn and rebellious" ways to being obedient to his commandments. The latest to do this was Jesus, who himself was foretold in the Book of Daniel and in the Book of Isaiah, where he is described as *Wonderful, Counselor, The Mighty God, The Everlasting Father, The Prince of Peace.*

But, instead of being listened to, Jesus, *the Prince of Peace*, wound up being killed. He said to accusers: *"Some of you are trying to kill me because my message doesn't find a home in your heart. You hear but don't understand, you look but don't see, for your hearts are fat and heavy."* To a woman, he said: *"Daughters of Jerusalem, don't weep for me, but for yourselves and your children. For if such things as these are done to me, the Living Tree, what will they do to you?"*

What was in the heart of the killers? The "yeast." It is what Jesus called the wrong teaching of the Pharisees and the Sadducees. Apostle Paul talked about this teaching in the Book of the Romans: *"For you are not real Jews just because you were born of Jewish parents or because you have gone through the Jewish initiation ceremony of circumcision. No, a real Jew is anyone whose heart is right with God. For God is not looking for those who cut their bodies in actual body circumcision, but he is looking for those with changed hearts and minds. Whoever has that kind of change in his life will get his praise from God."* He also said in the Philippians: *"Watch out for those wicked men—dangerous dogs, I call them-who say you must be circumcised to be saved. For it isn't the cutting of our bodies that makes us children of God; it is worshiping him with our spirits. That is the only true "circumcision." So I was a real Jew if there ever was one! What's more, I was a member of the Pharisees who demand the strictest obedience to every Jewish law and custom. And sincere? Yes, so much so that I greatly persecuted the church.*

But all these things that I once thought very worthwhile—now I've thrown them all away so that I can put my trust and hope in Christ alone. Yes, everything else is worthless when compared with the priceless gain of knowing Christ Jesus my Lord. For God's way of making us right with himself depends on faith—counting on Christ alone. Now I have given up everything else—I have found it to be the only way to really know Christ and to experience the mighty power that brought him back to life again, and to find out what it means to suffer and to die with him.

I have told you often before, and I say it again now with tears in my eyes, there are many who walk along the Christian road who are really enemies of the cross. Their future is eternal loss, for their god is their appetite. They are proud of what they should be ashamed of; and all they think about is this life here on earth. Think about things that are pure and lovely, and dwell on the fine good things others have."

The practice of circumcision is similar to the worship of icons by the church today. They are off the track of logic that I want to follow.

Thank you, Richard. Please pass along the word.

Sincerely,

Dan

P.S.: I'm attaching copies of all my correspondences . I hope you'll find them helpful.

* * * *

Richard came back with more questions. He said: I like the "communion" thing you just sent me, the *Come, Listen To Me*. It touched me with a sense of "oneness with the universe." But would you give me an example of idol worship? How does it compare to this "oneness thing?"

Dan's response:

I welcome your questions again.

The idol worship that I will discuss here came from the Exodus which tells the story about Moses leading his people to freedom from their long bondage in Egypt.

Along the way, before they reached their destination, Moses left his people for a moment to go up the mount (Mount Sinai) to confer with God, who gave him this edict:

I am Jehovah your God who liberated you from your slavery in Egypt.

You may worship no other god than me.

You shall not make yourselves any idols: any images resembling animals, birds or fish. You must never bow to an image or worship it in any way; for I, the Lord your God, am very possessive. I will not share your affection with any other god!

You shall not use the name of Jehovah your God irreverently, nor swear to falsehood.

Remember to observe the Sabbath Day.

Honor your father and mother.

You must not murder.

You must not commit adultery.

You must not lie.

You must not steal."

When Moses didn't come back from the mountain right away, the people went to Aaron, the older brother of Moses and first High Priest of the Hebrews. "Look," they said, "make us a god to lead us, for this fellow Moses who brought us here from Egypt has disappeared; something must have happened to him."

"Give me your golden earrings," Aaron replied.

So they all did—men and women, boys and girls. Aaron melted the gold, then molded and tooled it into the form of a calf. The people exclaimed, "O Israel, this is the god that brought you out of Egypt!"

When Aaron saw how happy the people were about it, he built an altar before the calf and announced, "Tomorrow there will be a fest to Jehovah!"

So they were up early the next morning and began offering burnt offerings and peace offerings to the calf idol; afterwards they sat down to feast and drink at a wild party, followed by sexual immorality..

Then the Lord told Moses, "Quick! Go on down, for your people that you brought from Egypt have defiled themselves, and have quickly aban-

doned all my laws. They have molded themselves a calf, and worshipped it, and sacrificed to it, and said, 'This is your god, O Israel, that brought you out of Egypt.' I have seen what a stubborn and rebellious lot these people are. Now let me alone and my anger shall blaze out against them and destroy them all." But Moses begged God not to do it, saying *"Remember your promise to your servants—to Abraham, Isaac, and Israel. For you swore by your own self, 'I will multiply your posterity as the stars of heaven, and I will give them all of this land I have promised to your descendants, and they shall inherit it forever.'"* So the Lord changed his mind and spared them. God could have dealt them one more blow (among many he had dealt them since Adam and Eve).

As a side note, a friend of mine asked me if God created Man or if Man created God. I reasoned that if God created Man, it begs questions as to why he created him and for what purpose. But if man created a god, like the golden calf, then his worship could only mirror his own values (like the wild parties and sexual immorality of the people of Aaron). The same questions can be asked about the use of statues or idols of all makes. They could only mirror ignorance and false understanding—the veil of misunderstanding. ("A material fallacy resulting from some prejudice.") They do not have a life in them, as Apostle Paul said. In other words, they lack the properties of the Spirit.

Through education, with the aid of computers and other modern means, may our understanding of the *Anointed One* increases. May our understanding of the Spirit change us and give us oneness in peace with ourselves and with our fellow men.

To get a better feel for this "oneness," I suggest you do what Diane did with *Come, Listen to Me*.

Thanks again for your question.

Sincerely,

Dan

Chapter 11

▼

Buster answered the doorbell to find a surprise.

Hi! Remember me?" he said, smiling but feeling intimidated.

"Why—of course! Julius! How ya, brother?" Buster said, as he puts out his hand to shake Julius'.

"What can we do for you?"

"I'd thought about this place," Julius said. "I'd like to talk to somebody."

"Sure. Come on in," Buster said. "Let's go outside. Dan and Betty are out there."

Julius followed Buster. As he stepped out into the verdant garden, he felt at home. Before they were his enemies, now they are his friends.

"Look who's here!" Buster announced.

"Julius!" Dan and Betty said, almost in unison. They went to hug him.

"You have a very nice place here," Julius said, shyly. He hadn't had a place to call home since his parents separated years ago. He became a drifter and slept anywhere he could lay his back on.

Julius lived in a world of "us against them." The "us" was an angry and hateful heart and an ignorant mind. He shared this world with the men he was with that night.

He was just a young teen when he was thrown in jail for assaulting a black man for no reason except hatred. The cross burning was his second brush with the law. They were just loafing around when they thought of robbing the nursery, but Buster and Betty caught their attention. Now, Julius is out of that world. Now he has a job and is back in school.

"Can I get you something?" Betty asked. "Coffee? Some breakfast?"

"No thank you. I'm just fine," Julius answered.

"Let us know if you need anything," Betty said. She and Buster left.

"I'd like to learn," Julius told Dan. "I was really impressed by you, folks, after meeting you the odd way. The name of this place alone intrigued me. It made me think."

"That's what we're here for," Dan said, "to give you something to think and feel about. But first, let me show you what we have here. Notice we have these booths that look out to the yard. Notice it's very quiet here. In a short while, I'll give you some bible passages for you to read and as you do so, look at a tree and try to feel its stillness. It's this peaceful feeling that I want you to get. Once you get it, you'll begin to understand these passages, or, at least, it would lend substance to them.

"If you have any questions, just note them down. We'll discuss them later. You may sit here for as long as you want. You may have lunch with us for a small donation, but we don't require it.

"You may disagree with us, but remember: We only want to help you and we hope you'd see us as a friend with a helping hand. I'll get the paper. I'll be right back."

Julius twiddled his thumbs while he waited. He stared outside but he saw nothing that excites him. So what? He thought. Dan came back. He had a piece of paper with him.

"I was expecting the big book," Julius said.

"No. Just a piece of paper with a few lines," Dan said, as he handed him the paper. "I trust that once you get the idea in it, the whole story will unfold to you sooner or later. You may start with the first one. Read it carefully as you look at a tree, and always be mindful of your feelings. Our purpose is to get your feelings attuned to the stillness and silence around here. This is sort of clearing the attic in your heart and mind. For a while they will rebel. But the tree won't budge, so to speak. Once in a while inhale deeply. Soon they'll come around and calm down. You'll feel peaceful and you see the tree clearly or objectively. When this happens the other passages will become understandable and meaningful. Got it?"

"I guess so," Julius said.

"Okay, call me when you need me," Dan said. He went back to the house to make copies of *Come, Listen To Me* and the others.

Julius started reading:

1) *It is the thought-life that pollutes. For from within, out of men's heart, come evil thoughts of lust, theft, murder, adultery, deceit, envy, lewdness, slander, pride, and all other folly.*

2) *I am in the Father and the Father is in me. The words I say are not my own but are from my Father who lives in me. But when the Father sends the Comforter instead of me—and by the Comforter I mean the Holy Spirit—he will teach you much, as well as remind you of everything I myself have told you. It is the source of all Truth. I am leaving you with a gift—a peace of mind and heart and the peace I give isn't fragile like the peace the world gives you.*
The heavens are made beautiful by the Spirit who gives intuition and instinct. Who is wise enough to number the stars? It is not age that makes man wise. Rather it is the Spirit in man, the breath of the Almighty which makes him intelligent.

3) *He will give you the inner strengthening of His Holy Spirit. May your roots go down, deep into the soil of God's marvelous love and may you be able to feel and understand as all children should.*

At the start, Julius was restless. All kinds of thoughts buzzed in his head. It's an attic alright, he thought. He sucked in the air deeply. He saw the tree the usual way, but his feeling wasn't involved. What's the point, he asked somewhat discouraged. But, at least, he was comfortable. He kept still. He noticed a bird alighting on a branch. He felt a touch. He caught himself. The kindness of the trio came to him. It touched him like he'd never been touched before. He saw the connection. Isn't this kindness, too? he asked. The bird must be tired and the tree gives it a place to rest on. Or if it's hungry, gives it something to eat. Why? These are acts of love and kindness! Now he saw kindness all-around him. The clean air he breathes gives life! Who set all these things up? It must be God! He must be very kind and loving. The realization stunned him into a deep silence. He was in awe like a child who has just discovered something.

"Hey, Dan! I'd like to talk to you!" Julius called out. Dan was in the garden looking things over as usual. He walked over to Julius.

"Yes, Julius," he said.

"I believe I understand the third passage. Actually, it grabbed me. It's awesome!

"Great! Congratulation!" Dan said. "The seed of the Spirit has just been planted in your heart. You've made your first step—like a baby's first. Number 2 will be your next step. Read it carefully like you did in step 1. You'll see that the statements '*The Father is in me…He will teach you much and reminds you of everything I myself have told you…It is the source of all Truth…Peace of mind*' refer to this Spirit that you've just discovered. This is what Apostle Paul meant when he said: '*Only those with the Holy Spirit with them can understand what the Holy Spirit means, and only those who have the Spirit of Christ can be called a Christian, for Christians actually do have within them a portion of the very thoughts and mind of Christ. If the great men of the world had had it they never would have crucified the Lord of Glory.*'

"But King Solomon gave this word of caution: '*God shows his anger from heaven against all sinful, evil men who push away the truth from them. For the truth about God is known to them instinctively. God has put this knowledge in their hearts. Claiming themselves to be wise without*

God, they became utter fools instead. And then, instead if worshiping the glorious, ever-living God, they took wood and stone and made idols for themselves, carving them to look like mere birds and animals and snakes and puny men.' The same warning is also told elsewhere: '*Woe to those who command their lifeless wooden idols to arise and save them, who call out to the speechless stone to tell them what to do. Can images speak for God? They are overlaid with gold and silver, but there is no breath at all inside. But the Lord is in his holy Temple; let all the earth be silent before him.'*

"Yes, Julius, you're stunned silent by the Holy Spirit. Now let this silence keep you straight and strong. Nurture it so that you won't lose it. Don't push it away. Continue to seek him. Here are some articles that will tell you more about the Spirit.

"Julius, it's been a pleasure having you with us."

"Thank you, Dan," Julius said. "It's more than a pleasure to me."

Chapter 12

▼

Dan answered the phone. It was George.

"Dan," he said, quietly. "Diane had just passed away."

"She passed away? Oh my God!" Dan gasped.

"Yes…" George said and paused, "she looked in her most peaceful when she did, as though she only went off to sleep."

"Yes," Dan said. "Diane had that. She had arrived at her most peaceful of moments. She told me in her last e-mail. God has blessed her with eternal peace. Is there anything I could do, George?"

"Yes. Please pray for her—oh, there's one thing," George said. "She mentioned a request before she died. She said something about some statements by Jesus, his apostle Paul and King Solomon. She wanted to know their meaning. She said her last day would be the best and she wanted something be said about it, like a beautiful song in a musical finale. I'd like you to do the eulogy. Perhaps you can use these statements for material. I'll send you the statements. I'll send the plane over to fetch you, Buster and Betty."

Dan felt humbled and honored by George's request. He accepted it, saying he'd do his best. Dan informed Buster and Betty. They, too, were very saddened.

There really isn't much communication among them, but in their private thoughts they pray for one another. They feel a special bond with one another.

Three days after receiving the news, an Airporter picked up Dan, Buster and Betty for the airport. Rick and Paula welcomed them aboard. After giving them instructions on the use of the jacket, she went to get their breakfast.

"Hmmm-mm! Man, I can't believe this!" a flabbergasted Buster said. He ran his fingers over the dark, buttery leather and pressed his foot into the thick velvet carpet. Dan was equally impressed, not because of the materials or the special treatment, but because of the meaning of all this. George is more than generous and loving. He believes in him and what he's doing. When he finished his food, he took out the eulogy from his jacket and went over it again. He worked on it well into the night the night before.

After two hours, the sleek, blue plane with *Where True Peace Lies* sliced through the Northwest gray autumn clouds, and in minutes made a touch down.

Dan, Buster and Betty thanked Rick and Paula as they stepped down the ladder to a waiting car. Jim, George personal driver, greeted them. Dan returned his greeting and introduced himself, Buster and Betty.

They were in no hurry to get to where they were going, but rather flowed leisurely with the heavy commuter traffic, through a floating bridge then to an island across a lake. Over the radio, Jim informed George they would be arriving shortly.

They followed a winding road lined with large homes with manicured lawns.

"Oh! How lovely!" Betty said, as thoughts of the Nevada desert crossed her mind.

"Yes, indeed," Buster said. "Hmmm-mm."

Jim turned into a wide driveway that led to three garages attached to a large, brick one-story. Jim stepped out to open Betty's door. He led them along granite walkway lined on both sides with multi-hued hedges, then stepped up into a brick alcove that curved into a pair of artistic wooden doors that gave the impression of welcoming arms. Jim pressed the doorbell. Almost instantly, they opened.

"Hi—there! Hi, Betty…Dan…Buster?" greeted George, smiling warmly but subdued. He hugged, first Betty then Buster then Dan. "Please, just feel at home," he said, as he led them through the foyer into a spacious living room. "Oh, let me take your coat, Betty," he said, as if he forgot a routine. He didn't use to that. Diane used to do that.

"Mark—would you come out here, please?" George called. "I want you to meet my friends." Mark, the cook and handyman, was in the kitchen preparing the snacks for their guests. He went out and shook hands with Dan and Buster. He touched cheeks with Betty.

"So, how was your trip?" George asked.

"Quite an experience," Dan said. "Very private and very special."

"Sure was. A private plane all our own for a coupla hours. Hmmm-mm!" Buster said.

"From pauper to princess—just fabulous!" Betty chimed in.

George, letting out what he felt, said: "Well—brothers and sister– I'm doing all these because you're my best friends. My best friend and my wife is gone. A family life is something I've missed all my life. I felt this when I was with you at the inaugural."

After chatting for a while with his friends, George excused himself. He wanted to make a call. He pointed at the wall of books, at the magazines and a newspaper and said: "There's plenty to read here. Just feel comfortable." He picked up a remote control box and pushed a button. A soft, classical music came floating in the air.

"Wow! How nice!" Betty said.

"Hmmm-mm," Buster cooed.

Betty read the paper and Buster just listened. Dan browsed through a book shelf and pulled out a book titled, *IT'S THE HEART THAT MATTERS*. He looked at the table of contents and picked out a chapter headed *Minting a Billionaire*.

A paragraph reads:

"After working a number of years for a software company, where he reaped a fortune from stock options and became a "Baby-Bill," George built his own computer company. It became very successful, so much so that a large conglomerate had to outbid a competitor to acquire it. He, then, invested heavily in cutting-edge technologies, among them the company that produced the cordless phone, later known as the 'cell phone.' He made a bundle on this one. He bankrolled a budding company that made re-usable rockets for space use. He helped develop the technology to decipher the genetic code. He financed a growing bio-tech industry and set up a program of study for it. As a sideline, he dabbled in real estate. He developed commercial properties, apartment buildings and homes when new residents from the other states came pouring in by the thousands. They were happenstances that timed so well with the dot-com boom. It minted George, the one-time poor boy, into a billionaire in the blink of an eye. For business and pleasure he bought and refurbished a Boeing 727. In spite of all these, however, it is the charitable work that matters to him. It is the heart that matters."

"*Purity is best generated by generosity,*" Dan recalled as he put the book down. He knew George has a rich life rather than a life of the rich. He knew he has a heart unmarred by arrogance, vanity and greed. They both believe this freedom as true freedom, the well from which strength, love and wisdom *gushes forth like a flowing river.* This is the kind of freedom Jesus had, he thought. It is the knot that binds them together as brothers and sister, and this could be the great knot that could tie all as one. It is one that is not carved in stone but in the human heart. This is the kind of freedom they want the world to see and have.

Dan likened George to Apostle Paul, who said: "*I have learned how to get along happily whether I have much or little. I know how to live on almost nothing or with everything. I have learned the secret of contentment in every situation, whether it be a full stomach or hunger, plenty or want;*

for I can do everything God asks me to with the help of Christ who gives me the strength and power."

By the time George came back, Mark had the drinks, fruits and sandwiches laid out on a table in the backyard.

The late morning sun came out and displayed that famous Northwest's autumn palette of beautiful white, gold, blue, red, green, pink and purple.

"Oh, how beautiful!" Betty mooned.

"Jobs and these colors bring people here," George said.

"And gambling and a boring blue bring people to Vegas," joked Dan.

"I like this one better. The heat out there is a little too much in the summer. Can I work for you?" Buster asked.

"Then who's gonna take care of the yard?" asked Betty, rehashing a playful retort.

"You will," said Buster. "You need the workout."

"Oh—you!" Betty said, tapping Buster's arm. They laughed. George loved the warm camaraderie. They helped themselves to the snacks.

"For more calories," George said, "this is our plan for the day. In a couple of hours, Jim will take you to the restaurant where I'll join you for lunch. After that, he'll take you home. Later on, in the evening, he will take you to the mortuary for the viewing. After that, he'll take you to a restaurant to join me, Diane's family and the rest of my crew. After that, he'll take you home to get ready for tomorrow."

When they were done with their snacks, George left to attend to some business. Dan, Buster and Betty sat around for a while then retired to their rooms for a rest. A few hours later, Jim arrived as planned. He took them to have lunch with George. After that, he took them home. Later in the evening, he took them to the funeral home.

The Home was located some distance outside of town. They were among the first to arrive. George led them to the lectern to sign the visitors' book. Dan signed in first, then Buster then Betty. They joined George, who was now standing by the casket.

As Dan looked at reposed Diane, a train of thoughts crossed his mind: There is a time to be born, a time to die...A time to lose, a time to find...From dust she came, to dust she shall return and her Spirit returns to God...Death conquers the body but not the Spirit...Who would know the meaning of death?...You could move a mountain into the sea if you have faith...He is the Christ...The Messiah...I am the light and the resurrection...He rose from the dead...And the last day I will cause all such to rise from the dead...Yes, Diane, you will rise."

When they were done viewing, Dan, Buster and Betty went to hug George.

"I'm very sorry," Betty said, as she held George's hand and looked into his eyes. George looked back into hers, intently but leisurely. "Thank you, Betty, *there's a time to lose,*" he said and returned her hug.

George went to greet Diane's parents Bill and Susan, and their friends and relatives. They have just walked in. They talked a bit then proceeded to the coffin. George followed them. They nestled closely into one another, their heads bowed. Sobs and sniffles took over the quiet room. George wrapped his arm around her mother-in-law's shoulders to comfort her. He stood by her then, when she was done, helped her to her chair.

George went to get Dan, Buster and Betty to introduce to them. Bill and Susan are schoolteachers. Susan also teaches Sunday school. Diane was their only child. They offered their condolences to them, chatted a bit about the weather then politely withdrew. They wanted them to have more time with their son-in-law.

George started to discuss Diane's spirituality but he held his tongue when Susan said: "So that's the man who put this stuff into Diane's head and yours." He knew she didn't like Dan. He knew it the first time he talked to her about the subject.

"Dan will talk more about this spirituality in his eulogy tomorrow," George said. "You'll like it."

"We'll see," she said.

When all the mourners had left, George spent a few moments with Diane. He wanted to feel the "oneness with her" in total silence.

George drove home alone along the lonely winding road. He thought about Susan. A veil of misunderstanding covers her heart and mind, George thought. He knew she did ask questions, yet she just didn't like Diane's new dress of spirituality. How could she, he thought. She is a creature of habit, and this one habit doesn't like strangers. Not so with Diane, he thought. She was a child who saw her world openly, simply, honestly and joyously. She saw the truth. But this truth is a stranger to her mom.

When he got home, he found Dan working on the eulogy.

"Hi, Dan—are you ready for tomorrow?" George asked.

"Not quite. I'm going over it one more time. Any suggestion?" Dan asked.

"Wait," George said, "I just remembered. I had this talk with Susan sometime ago. I got it in the computer. I'll make a copy for you." George left. A half-hour later, he came back with the copy.

Dan looked it over. "Hey, I like it," he said. "The folks raised good questions and I like your answers. I couldn't have done better. I'll use it."

"Good night, Dan."

"Good night, George."

* * * *

The room hushed when Dan stepped up to the lectern to deliver the eulogy. He looked over everyone for a second then began:

"Diane was beautiful woman. She was a true beauty in the eyes of the Lord.

She said her last day would be the best day of her life. She wanted to celebrate it like, as she put it, a beautiful song in a musical finale. This song is in the form of an answer to a question she asked.

Just before she died, she wanted to know the meaning of some statements made by Jesus, his apostle Paul and the wise man, King Solomon.

George suggested I use the answers for her eulogy. I hope we meet her wish.

These are the statements:

Jesus: *Those the Father speaks to, who learn the truth from him, will be attracted to me...I am in the Father and the Father is in me...Only the Holy Spirit gives eternal life...And the Last Day I will cause all such to rise again from the dead.*

Apostle Paul: *God had put his brand upon us—his mark of ownership—and given us his Holy Spirit in our hearts as guarantee that we belong to him, and as first installment of all that he is going to give us.*

King Solomon: *From dust we came, to dust we shall return and the Spirit returns to God.*

To understand a key word here is to understand the meaning of these statements. The word is the "Spirit." It is described as "A divine animating influence or inspiration." Let me give you an example of this. I'll read to you a composition I gave to Diane. It's titled *Come, Listen To Me*. Imagine a Tree talking to Diane. It said:

Look at me carefully. Take your time. I am patient.

See me for what I really am, and you'll find that I am more than what you think I am.

Notice and feel my stillness. Hear and feel my silence, and you'll do away the confusion in your mind and becalm your troubled heart, just as I clean the air you breathe.

I am in you and you are in me and the rest of the garden under the sun and the stars. I am, as you are, with the seasons. I am pure in spirit.

I give you flowers to enjoy in the spring and a shade for your summer respite. I give you colors in the fall. I give you beauty that is natural. I have the fortitude to withstand the winter storms, for my roots are anchored firmly in the soil, like my faith in my Creator. I give you Love and Life. That is my only purpose for being.

I stand here without judgment about you. Come and listen to me. Give me your thoughts and feelings and I'll give them back cleansed with the spirit of peace and love that's God's, that's in me.

She told me how the Tree animated and inspired her. This is what she said:

'Thank you for your *Come, Listen To Me*. It was really something. It helped me in a very unique way.

Just lately, I have been going through a lot of pain, fear and anxiety. It was only this morning when George and I went outside in our backyard with copies in our hands. We sat side by side in our patio, facing the blooming trees and the water. Beside us were these lovely pots of flowers. The sun was coming up from behind us, washing our garden and the lake with a delightfully cool, soft brilliance. Oh! What a magnificent morning!

Magnificent—yet impersonal and indifferent! But then as I silently read *Come, Listen To Me* and rubbed a soft petal gently between my fingers, something very unusual happened. The tree and everything around me became a new experience. A new awareness came to me, as if a film peeled suddenly off my eyes. I felt as if I was outside of my self and became as one with them. I was totally free! Free from fear, anxiety and my pain-wracked body! I felt light as the light that surrounded me! Oh! What a glorious a feeling!

George told me that the peace he also felt was so deep it reached down to the very root of his guilt feeling. It gave him a strong feeling of self-control.

And you know what? I learned a lesson, too. It judged me not whether I am a Jew or a Gentile, a Protestant or a Catholic, a Buddhist or a Muslim, a black or white, a brown or yellow. It makes no difference to the tree! It makes no difference to God at all!"

Yes, Diane was divinely animated and inspired: Jesus' statements—*Those the Father speaks to, who learn the truth from him, will be attracted to me...I am in the Father and the Father is in me*—are, in spirit, the same as these statements: "I am in you and you are in me and the rest of the garden under the sun and the stars. I am, as you are, with the seasons. I am pure in spirit." She felt she was outside of her self and, yes, she became as one with her surroundings.

This moment of peace and freedom that Diane had was God's first installment of the Spirit, an installment for the eternal life.

Now we ask: who is God? How could we know? Let me give you another example.

Last night George gave me a copy of a discussion he had with Bill and Susan, his parents-in-law.

Susan told George: "I don't quite get what you're telling me about this spirituality thing. During the time she was ill, she rarely mentioned the word 'God' to me. You know, God's the third three-letter word she learned from us after 'mom' and 'dad,' but she'd pretty much dropped it out of her vocabulary. God controls everything. Everything is in his name. Without God nothing works. Yet, I reckon, not once did she mention God. She didn't even talk about praying. We taught her how to pray when she was little, so we wondered how else could she have received grace from our almighty God if she didn't pray? Praying could have helped her."

George replied: "Yes, I agree. But she did pray, and prayed with the same deep and sincere feeling as when she was little. This feeling is love—love for you and Bill and, as far as this feeling went during her tender years, 'Mom,' 'Dad' and 'God' are all one and the same. She lumped them all together when she told you, 'I love you.' Later on in life, this love translated into true faith and an understanding that, I believe, couldn't have come by searching for the big picture. For who would know about the complex whole or the Great Equation? This is the domain of God that only Jesus knew. Now, as an adult, all she knew was in the lower rung of this equation ladder. They are the meaningful little words 'love,' 'mom' and 'dad,' and the feelings associated with them—feelings that were rekindled or inspired by the Tree. The words of the Tree were the words of the Spirit that were written in her heart. It is through her heart she found God back. Yes, through her heart. This is Jesus way, the way to get us back to the Garden of Eden and to the Eternal Life. This is the understanding of God she wanted to pass on to us all."

"*From dust she came, to dust she shall return and her spirit returns to God,*" said King Solomon.

"*I am the light and the resurrection. At the last day I will cause all to rise from the dead,*" said Jesus.

'I felt light as the light that surrounded me!' Diane proclaimed, as if she had just heard a beautiful song. The song was the light that shined inside her soul. She has risen."

* * * *

At the cemetery, George, Dan, Buster and Betty stayed after everyone had left. They waited for the moment. Like George did in the funeral home when the mourners were gone, they stood before Diane with their heads bowed. They stood as still and silent as the trees, as still and silent as she, and became as one in Spirit with her. They stood silently with her in the *Holy Temple of God*. This was their last farewell.

* * * *

Jim drove Dan, Buster and Betty back to the airport for their return flight home. They got snared in the heavy traffic. They were boxed in. Nothing moved. They were glad their ride waited for them, though. He called Rick to inform him they would be late.

"You know what this reminds me of?" Dan said. "It reminds me of the buggy race in the Friendly Persuasion. I love the movie. It was a picture of a time and place when 'freeway' meant just that, not as it means today: multiple lanes and fully controlled like we are in right now. No such controls then and whoever leaves the dust on the other driver's face won the race.

"Then, life's ambience was spiritual. There, inside the church, the people took turns reciting biblical verses. They sang and prayed against the backdrop of a beautiful surrounding and whether they were aware of it or not, the beauty of the land gave spiritual substance to their sayings. It was the time of the civil war, and this spirituality came into play in their fight.

"So it did to the Indians in earlier times. Today, they are called the 'Soul of America'. The desire they pursued was more basic than the 'pursuit of happiness' that was pursued by their pursuers. Theirs, like the church-goers,' went deeper in the heart.

"'This is a good day to die,' an Indian chief said before the battle that had cost him his life. It must have been a helluva beautiful day. It fired him up to fight. This tells about the heart of the man—a heart molded, not by the bible but by the beauty of the land. So when they lost their land they lost that spirit, too. Now look what had became of them. No amount of dole-outs could replace that spirit. We may not know or care much about that, but all of us are now on the same boat. Here we are, stuck on this freeway and contributing to the loss of this spiritual ambience. One day we may wake up to find all is gone, gone and learn but too late what the Bible says:

'And if riches are desired in life, what is richer than wisdom which is responsible for all things? And if perception is effective, who accomplishes more than wisdom which designs what exists? And if a man loves justice, wisdom's labor have great virtue; for it teaches temperance, prudence, justice and courage, which are the most valuable things men can have in life. And if a man desires much knowledge, it knows things past and foretells what is to come; it knows the subtleties of speeches, and the solutions of arguments; it knows signs and wonders before they are done, and the outcome of times and ages.'"

"That's interesting," Jim said. "Well, we're here—finally."

Rick and Paula welcomed them onboard. Paula took a large rose bouquet from Betty and stowed it away. An envelope was attached to it. It came from George.

Two hours later, they arrived home. Buster offered to carry the flowers down the steps, but Betty said no. She didn't let anybody carry it but her. Dan and Buster looked at each other and smiled knowingly. They understood how she felt.

When they arrived home, Betty opened the envelope and read the note: "Thank you for being around in my hour of sadness. *There's time to find.*" There seemed to be a missing part. Later on, it dawned on her: *There's time to lose.* She puts them together: *There's time to lose... There's time to find.*"

Betty replied with a Thank You letter.

"Dear George," it begun. "The rose bouquet was just beautiful and your note filled me with joy and hope. It was a time for crying, but there will be a time for dancing and laughing."

George replied by e-mail: "Yes, there will be."

Chapter 13

A question came in from Alfonso of Mexico. He said he had heard about Dan from a friend.

"Please tell me," Alfonso asked. "Why did Jesus say, just ask for anything in his Name and his Father will give it? Why did the Bible say, keep on praying and you will keep on getting? Isn't this good enough."

Dans's answer:

Yes, they are good and very powerful, too, if for instance, the following example is true. It came from a little book titled *The Wonders of the Holy Name*.

Quote: "In the year 1274 evils threatened the world. The Church was assailed by fierce enemies from within and without. So great was the danger that the Pope, Gregory X, who then reigned, called a council of Bishops in Lyons to determine on the best means of saving society from the ruin that menaced it. Among the many means proposed, the Pope and Bishops chose what they considered the easiest and most efficacious of all, viz., the frequent repetition of the Holy Name of Jesus.

The Holy Father then begged the Bishops of the world and their priests to call on the Name of Jesus and to urge their peoples to place all their confidence in this all–powerful Name, repeating it constantly with boundless trust. The Pope entrusted the Dominicans especially with the glorious task of preaching the wonders of the Holy Name in every country, a work they accomplished with unbounded zeal....Their efforts were crowned with success so that the enemies of the Church were overthrown, the dangers that threatened society disappeared and peace once more reigned supreme.

This is a most important lesson for us because in these our own days, dreadful sufferings are crushing many countries, and still greater evils threaten all the others.

No government or governments seem strong and wise enough to stem this awful torrent of evils. There is but one remedy, and that is *prayer*.

Every Christian must turn to God and ask Him to have mercy on us. The easiest of all prayers, as we have seen, is the Name of Jesus.

Everyone without exception can invoke this holy name hundreds of times a day, not only for his own intentions, but also to ask God to deliver the world from impending ruin.

It is amazing what one person who prays can do to save his country and save society. We read in Holy Scripture how Moses saved by his prayer the people of Israel from destruction, and how one pious woman, Judith of Betulia, saved her city and her people when the rulers were in despair and about to surrender themselves to their enemies.

Again, we know that the two cities of Sodom and Gomorrha, which God destroyed by fire for their sins and crimes, would have been pardoned had there been only ten good men to pray for them!

Over and over again we read of kings, emperors, statesmen and famous military commanders who placed all their trust in prayer, thus working wonders. If the prayers of one man can do much, what will not the prayers of many do?

The Name of Jesus is the shortest, the easiest and most powerful of prayers. Everyone can say it, even in the midst of his daily work. God cannot refuse to hear it.

Let us then invoke the Name of Jesus, asking him to save us from the calamities that threaten us."

A magic wand, this praying and calling His Name it seems like, isn't it? But whatever works, I'd say—but let me ask: Why was Jesus killed? Why did he let this thing happen to him, when all he could have done was pray and wiped his tormentors off the face of the earth? And why did his accusers hate him?

"*Crucify him!*" they shouted.

"*Why? What has he done wrong?*" Pilate demanded, but they kept shouting, "*Crucify! Crucify!*"

In regard to the first and second questions, some religion says that there is this God's plan that "Jesus would die to wash away all the sins of men." This tells me that all sinners, including his crucifiers, would be forgiven, regardless. Granted. But why did Jesus tell a woman: "*Daughters of Jerusalem, don't weep for me, but for yourselves and your children. For if such things as these are done to me, the Living Tree, what will they do to you?*" Moreover, why did Apostle Paul say: "*I advise you to obey only the Holy Spirit's instruction. He will tell you where to go and what to do, and then you won't always be doing the wrong things your evil nature wants you to. For we naturally love to do evil things that are just the opposite from the things that the Holy Spirit tells us to do; and the good things we want to do when the Spirit has its way with us are just the opposite of your natural desires. These two forces within us are constantly fighting each other to win control over us, and our wishes are never free from their pressures.*" In light of these statements, it seems pointless to say that we, sinners, are forgiven. So what's the point? Apostle Paul made it clear. He tells us to do away with our natural desires or take control of them. And to do this we need to obey or seek the help of the Spirit. This is not in the same sense as "washing all sins of men," or being forgiven is it?

In regard to the question why Jesus was hated by his accusers, Apostle Paul said:

"*Their future is eternal loss for their god is their appetite. They are proud of what they should be ashamed of, and all they could think about is this life here on earth.*" Jesus went against their lifestyle and they hated him for it. They killed him because of it.

He leadeth me by the still water. He comforteth me, the 23rd Psalm said. Jesus leading us the way to salvation through the Holy Spirit is not the same thing as being forgiven. Rather, it's telling us to follow him.

Again, Apostle Paul said: "*You are now controlled by your new nature because the Spirit of God is in now living in you. Only those with the Holy Spirit with them can understand what the Holy Spirit means, and only those who have the Spirit of Christ can be called a Christian, for Christians actually do have within them a portion of every thought and mind of Christ. But the great men of the world have not understood it. If they had had it they never would have crucified the Lord of Glory.*

The prophet Simeon of Jerusalem told Mary, the mother of Jesus: "*A sword shall pierce your soul, for this child shall be rejected by many in Israel, and this to their own undoing. But he will be the greatest joy of many others. And the deepest thoughts of many hearts shall be revealed.*" What a price to pay for hatred and ignorance.

"*I want you to know me,*" Jesus said. I would rather do that by following logic than doing the yeast, the statues or the name-calling mantra of the Dark ages. I hope my correspondences that I'm attaching here show that.

Thank you, Alfonso. Please pass the word around and continue to be in touch.

Sincerely,

Dan

* * * *

A question came in from Natasha of Russia. She wants to know what Dan's thoughts are on Spirituality and Freedom.

Dan's reply:

From Biblical times forward, Spirituality and Freedom have journeyed hand-in-hand. The struggle for one was also the struggle for the other. The struggle of Jesus, as a man, is a classic example of this. It was a struggle both inside and outside of him. Inside, it was the battle of the Spirit against human nature. Outside, it was the battle of his Spirit against the tyranny during his time.

About his enemy inside, he said: *"It is the thought-life that pollutes. For from within, out of men's hearts, come evil thoughts of lust, theft, murder, adultery, wicked ness, envy, lewdness, slander, pride, and all other folly."* They are the satans inside us that would lead us to foolishness, destruction and (spiritual) death.

"I am from A to Z, the beginning and the end, the First and the Last. Cheer up! I have overcome the world!" he declared triumphantly. So he won both his struggles inside and outside of him. He feared nothing including death. He had total self-control. He was free from the satans. This is the kind of freedom he wanted to give to the world. This is the message we want the world to know.

This is the freedom that Apostle meant when he wrote: *"So Christ has made us free. Now make sure you stay free and don't bet all tied up again in the chains of slavery. For we naturally love to do evil things that are just the opposite from the things that the Holy Spirit tells us to do; and the good things we want to do when the Sprit has his way with us are just the opposite of our natural desires. But when you follow your own wrong inclinations your lives will produce these evil results: impure thoughts, eagerness for lustful pleasures, idolatry, hatred and fighting, jealousy and anger, complaints and criticisms, feeling that everyone else is wrong except those in your own little group-and there will be wrong doctrine, envy, murder and all that sort of thing. But when the Holy Spirit controls our lives he will produce this kind of fruit in us: love, joy, peace, kindness, goodness, faithfulness, gentleness and self-control. Those who belong to Christ have nailed their natural evil desires to his cross and crucified them there."*

Where did Jesus get his spiritual strength to overcome his enemies with?

1) Not from the worship of idols or obedience to the customs and rules during his time. "*They seem good,*" Apostle Paul said about them, "*For they require strong devotion but have no effect in conquering evil thoughts and desires. They only make the worshipper proud.*

2) Not from the Ten Commandments. Even these are not good enough. The New Testament or Covenant had this to say: "*The old way, trying to be saved by keeping the Ten Commandments, ends in death; in the new way, the Holy Spirit gives them life. Yet, that old system of law began with such glory that people could not bear to look at Moses' face though it was already fading away. In fact, that first glory as it shone from Moses' face was worth nothing at all in comparison with the overwhelming glory of the new agreement* (with the Spirit of Jesus*). Since we know that this new glory will never go away, we can preach with great boldness, and not as Moses did, who put a veil over his face so that the Israelis could not see the glory fade away. Not only Moses' face was veiled, but his people's minds and understanding were veiled and blinded too. Even now when the Scripture is read it seems as though Jewish hearts and minds are covered by a thick veil, because they cannot see and understand the real meaning of the Scriptures. Yes, even today when they read Moses' writings their hearts are blind and they think that obeying the Ten Commandments is the way to be saved. This veil of misunderstanding can be removed only by believing in Christ.*"

3) Not from ceremonial baptism of circumcision. Apostle Paul said: "*When you came to Christ he set you free from your evil desires, not by a*

bodily operation of circumcision but a spiritual operation, the baptism of your souls. For in baptism you see how your old, evil nature died with him and was buried with him and came out of death with him into a new life."

Where did Jesus get it then? Answer: From an experience akin to those of Diane's and Betty's. I'm sending you copies of their experiences along with a copy of *Come Listen To Me*. I'm also sending a copy of Dan's discussion with Betty regarding Jesus confronting the temptations by Satan in the wilderness.

Please feel free to ask if you have any more questions.

Sincerely,

Dan

*   *   *   *

From Hungary came this question from Jen: Could you give me examples of prophesies and actual events that correspond to them? Could you give me an example of history repeating itself?

Dan's reply:

I like your questions, Jen. Here are some examples:

Prophesies (This one came from Isaiah.): *"For unto us a Child is born; unto us a Son is given; and the government shall be upon his shoulder. These will be his royal titles: Wonderful, Counselor, The Mighty God, The Everlasting Father, The Prince of Peace. His government was upon his shoulder.* He would be made to suffer and die.

This other prophesy came from the Book of Daniel: *Then I, Daniel, looked and saw two men on each bank of a river. And one of them asked the man in a linen robe who was standing now above the water, "How long will it be until all terrors end?"*

He replied with both hands lifted to heaven, taking oath by him who lives forever and ever, that they will not end until three and a half years after the power of God's people are crushed.

I heard what he said but I didn't understand what he meant, so I said, "Sir, how will this all come out?"

But he said, "Go now, Daniel, for what I have said is not to be understood until the time of the end. Many shall be purified by great trials and persecutions. But the wicked shall continue in their wickedness, and none of them will understand. It will not be understood until the end times, when travel and education shall be vastly increased. And even then only those who are willing to learn will know what it means." Guess who the man in the white robe was? It was Jesus.

History repeating itself: (This also came from Isaiah.) *"Woe to Jerusalem, the city of David. Year after year you make your many offerings, but I will send heavy judgment upon you and there will be weeping and sorrow. For Jerusalem shall become as her name "Ariel" means—an altar covered with blood. I will be your enemy. I will surround Jerusalem and lay siege against it, and build forts around it to destroy it.*

Your voice will whisper like a ghost from the earth where you lie buried.

But suddenly your ruthless enemies will be driven away like chaff before the wind. In an instant, I the Lord of Hosts, will come upon them with thunder, earthquake, whirlwind and fire. And all the nations fighting Jerusalem will vanish like a dream!

You are amazed, incredulous? You don't believe it? Then go ahead and be blind if you must! You are stupid—and not from drinking, either! Stagger, and not from wine. For the Lord has poured out upon you a spirit of deep sleep. He has closed the eyes of your prophets and seers, so all these future events are a sealed book to them."

What do think, Jen? Don't they sound like today's news? They are accurate almost to the point, aren't they?

It's a pleasure discussing with you. Would you help pass the word around?

Sincerely,

Dan

*   *   *   *

From Milagros of the Philippines came this question: Is the vision told by Jesus in the Revelation possible? It seems like Jesus had a case of bad flu when this nightmarish vision appeared to him.

Dan's answer: Yes—it is possible, as unimaginable as it might seem to the rest of us. Perhaps, the closest we might get to it is a bad dream when we have a bad flu, like you said. But Jesus was not dreaming. Let's be logical, he said. But does this total nightmare follow logically from anything he did or said? I can't think of a thing. But we've all heard the word "hell." Now let's consider what could be a logical opposite to it. How about Heaven? Yes, we've heard that one, too. Now let's ask: if there is a heaven, could there be a hell, too? Yes, logically speaking. Therefore, I think the vision of Jesus in the Revelation is a vision of hell.

If God could create something out of nothing, he certainly could make the "unreal," real. Only God knows what we can never know. Jesus had God's mind. He had *seen* God. He was the Spirit. He was the Son of God. He was God.

I hope I've answered your question. Please spread the Word.

Sincerely,

Dan

* * * *

Weeks then months passed by. Dan continued to receive questions and give answers to them. He sent articles to newspapers and magazines but heard nothing back from them. He pushed on.

Then, one day, as if out of the blue, came a surprise message. It came from George. It said: "Dan, I had a dream last night. I dreamt of Bobby then Diane then Betty. They were mere glimpses but man! were they beautiful and very real! They left me feeling very sad. I couldn't get Bobby and Diane back but Betty is here. You know what I mean—don't you? What do you think?"

Dan's reply: "I understand, George. Dreams are like spirituals, I mean they dwell deep in us. I believe Betty has this deep thing, too. I could tell she has also seen this beauty. Now, she even calls us 'her boys,' and leads us in prayers before meals. She is a fine woman. Why just dream of her? Go for it!"

George also asked Buster's advice. Buster didn't give an advice, but divined: "You'll make a beautiful couple, George. Hmmm-mm."

Chapter 14

An e-mail came in for Buster from a minister in the valley. It said:

"I've read about the cross-burning some time ago. I've also heard about your place Where True Peace Lies. My parish would love to meet you. I look forward with hope."

Sincerely yours,

Reverend James
The Inn of Fellowship in Christ

* * * *

Buster showed the message to Dan.

"Alright!" said Dan. "Go for it. Go tell 'em!"

"Yeah—but…" Buster hesitated, then said timidly, "the only time I ever spoke seriously was before a judge and the parole board. Ya know what I mean?"

"I understand. Don't worry about it. Just relax. Think of the peaceful things—a tree—you know," Dan said. "I'll help you write it."

"Okay, I'll go," Buster said. Buster accepted the invitation. Dan and Betty would go, too, to root for him.

Dan printed out pamphlets of all his correspondences (including Julius' and the eulogy). He planned to distribute them to the churchgoers. He sent a copy to George.

* * * *

The Inn was located in a neighborhood noted for drugs and crimes. Reverend James, in a white and purple robe, greeted them as they came in. They, including their children, were all dressed up in their Sunday best. Dan could see how a parish community could very well be a force for good in the community. It is *the* bright spot, he thought. He saw the solution.

"Reverend James, I'm Buster. How are you?" Buster said, as he puts his hand out to shake the Reverend's. Reverend James was a cheerful old man who had served his parish a long time.

"Buster! Why—my prayer has been answered! How are you, son?" the Reverend said.

"Fine, Reverend. It's a beautiful day. I'd like you to meet Dan and Betty," Buster said.

"Oh, what a lovely couple! Happy to have you with us," Reverend James said.

"We're all friends to each other," Buster said.

"Oh—I see," the Reverend said and shook Dan's and Betty's hands.

* * * *

Dan, Buster and Betty sat in the back of the large, nicely decorated room. It was filled to capacity that morning.

A woman took to the lectern and asked everyone to turn to a page in the hymnal. She led the singing. Above the pounding organ, they sang energetically and clapped their hands. Dan thought about the wickedness in the streets at night. He didn't see the good winning over the evil.

After they had done a few songs, Reverend James took his turn.

"Good morning," he begun. "I'm happy to see you all again. Here with us this morning are our friends Buster, Dan and Miss Betty. They are from a garden retreat in the northwest part of town. It is called Where True Peace Lies. I like what I heard about it. Let's welcome them!" He pointed a finger towards the back. The congregation stood up and turned their heads towards them and clapped their hands.

"Brother Buster will give us a talk," the Reverend said. "Welcome, brother, we're proud to have you here with us."

Buster walked up to the lectern, spread out a couple of sheets on it and began:

"I'm happy to be here. They call me Buster. Ya know—I used to bust folks. I used to live in a mean world like you see out here at night. But I'm now a different man. Inside, I'm like a child. Yes—sir!

"The Inn of Fellowship in Christ. A beautiful name. It reminds me of a story about an Inn whose door was slammed shut to Mary, Joseph and their newborn child Jesus that one winter night. There was no room for them, not even a tiny corner for the child, perhaps because they had no means to pay their way in. So, out there, baby Jesus lay on a mattress of hay. It was a cold night. But man's heart was much colder.

"Fellowship in Christ means Love and Mercy. It is the Spirit of Jesus. It is the Rock Foundation upon which his church was built. Let this be the same Rock upon which our personal foundation is built.

"Let's identify with it. Let it be our new Identity. Let it be our own source of strength.

'Don't copy the behavior and customs of this world, but be a new and different person with a fresh newness in all you do and think,' so Apostle Paul said. He's telling us to get rid of the image and name others have given us, or we think they have given us. Let's get rid of them. They only make us weak. Let our new identity now be our I's.

Where do find it? We won't hear it on TV. We won't hear it in the schools or even in the churches. Where do we find it? You're hearing it right now: You'll find it in God's beautiful creation. You'll find it in nature. You'll find it in the beautiful flowers and trees in your garden. You'll find it when you feel the silence that goes down deep inside your hearts, a silence that gives you strength and confidence. This is the weapon you need to fight the disturbances in you and outside of you. This is the way to bring out the new and different 'I' or person in you. This is the idea behind Where True Peace Lies. Come visit us one day and we'll show you.

"Thank you, Reverend James. Thank you all."

Reverend James went back to the lectern to thank Buster for his "eloquent and most thoughtful message," and to announce that pamphlets containing answers and questions regarding Where True Peace Lies would be given on their way out.

The service continued.

Dan and Betty congratulated Buster.

"That's very good, Buster," Dan whispered as he shook Buster's hand. "Much better than the one we worked on together."

"I love it. Hmmm-mm!" Betty said, imitating Buster's cooing.

"Thanks. It came from the heart." Buster said. He was enjoying it all.

* * * *

Dan, Buster and Betty arrived home to find a message in their computers. It came from George. It read: "I plan to marry one of you guys. What do you think?"

Dan replied: "I don't think so. I'd rather not get involve in that sort of thing. I'm an ascetic, you know. Did you mean Buster?"

But it wasn't Buster, either. "Who-me? Na-ah!" he said. So that left Betty. "Oh, my Gosh!" she exclaimed, as if she had just won a lottery. She snatched a copy and rushed off to verify with Dan and Buster.

"I believe so," Dan said. "You have my recommendation."

"I gave him mine, too," Buster said. "You deserve it, kido."

Betty was enrapt. She hugged them, as tears welled in her eyes. A while later, Betty went back to her computer. The proof came in. "Betty—will you marry me?"

Chapter 15

The wedding took place at the Chapel-by-the-Lake the following spring. As the proxy father, Dan gave away Betty. Buster was the Best Man.

It was a simple but an elegant wedding, with only a few invited guests. It was like a fairy tale. Betty, the Cinderella, married a Prince with the help of a fairy godfather. Dan was the godfather.

They celebrated the wedding aboard Bobby, George's yacht named after his kid brother. They sailed around Puget Sound and feasted on a Pacific Northwest fare: Broiled Copper River salmon and boiled King and Dungeness crabs.

*   *   *   *

Dan had an e-mail waiting for him when he and Buster arrived home from the wedding. It came from Betty, thanking him for everything. She called Dan his guardian angel. But Dan deflected the credit back to her by e-mail that if there was one thing that stood out of all this, it was that she had done it for herself when she *chose* to join him.

Dan told her the biblical story of Tobit, a kind man, who, before he became blind, went out of his way to help others.

He copied the Bible:

He performed many good deeds to his relatives and his people. When saw a body thrown outside the walls of Nineveh, he would bury it.

Tobit wishes in life came true. Among them was a wish for his son Tobias to find a wife. Tobias did find one but she was bewitched. Seven husbands died on their first day with her. But a friend, who turned out to be an angel named Raphael, saved his life and their marriage turned a happy one. Raphael also guided Tobias safely in a long journey.

As always, Tobit was kind. By the deed of the same angel, Tobit sight was restored and a bevy of grand-and great-grandchildren were borne for him.

Dan also told her the story of Job who was rewarded for his infinite patience and faith in God, just as Tobit was rewarded for his kindness.

Again, Dan copied the Bible:

God even let Satan put Job to test. He asked Satan: 'Have you noticed my servant Job? He is the finest man in all earth—a good man who fears me and will have nothing to do with evil.'

'Why shouldn't he, when you pay him so well?' Satan scoffed. 'You have always protected him and his home and his property from all harm. You helped him prosper in everything he does—look how rich he is! No wonder he worships you! But just take away his wealth and you'll see him curse you to your face!'

And the Lord replied to Satan, 'You may do anything you like with his wealth, but don't harm him physically.' So Satan went away; and sure enough, not long afterwards when Job's sons and daughters were dining at the oldest brother' house, tragedy struck.

A messenger rushed to Job's home with this news: 'Your oxen were plowing, with the donkeys feeding beside them, when the Sabeans raided us, drove away the animals and killed all the farmhands except me. Then fire from God has fallen from heaven and burned up your sheep and all the herdsmen and I alone have escaped to tell you.'

Many more tragedies befell on Job, but he did not turn his back on his Lord. In the end, The Lord blessed him more than the beginning. For now he had 14,000 sheeps, 6,000 camels. He lived 140 years, living to see his grandchildren and great-grandchildren too. Then at last he died, an old, old man, after having lived a good life.

Dan told Betty that if she hadn't stayed the course, God wouldn't have rewarded her just as he had rewarded Tobit and Job.

"Stay simple and elegant for George," he said, "Buster and I will surely miss your simple and elegant dishes, too."

* * * *

Dan was aware he was giving the impression that Betty's blessings came as predictable results, as if from the Great Equation. God cranks it up and out comes the answer.

He knew that in real life things don't always work out that way. He asked: what if Betty wound up with a bum? Or if she hadn't changed, wound up with a Prince just the same? Would it matter, then, if she hadn't changed? Yes, it would have, he thought. She would have been a fool who *starts with a premise that concludes in sheer madness and brings her ruin.* That's for sure, he thought.

Dan understood Apostle Paul when he said: "*Stop fooling yourselves. If you count yourselves above in intelligence, as judged by the world's standards, you had better put this all aside and be a fool rather than let it hold you back from the true wisdom from above. For the wisdom of this world is foolishness to God. As it says in the book of Job, God uses man's own brilliance to trap him; he stumbles over his own 'wisdom' and falls. And again in the book of Psalms, we are told that the Lord knows full well how the human mind reasons, and how foolish and futile it is.*"

"Yes," Dan thought, "Just like what happened to me when I lost everything, Betty's 'brilliance' would have trapped her, too. She would have stumbled over her 'wisdom' and fell." But they both learned their lessons. They changed because of the seed of the Spirit that was planted in them.

Dan knew the Bible referred to this: "*Why, we're just God's servants, and with our help you believed. My work was to plant the seed in your hearts, and Apollos' work was to water it, but it was God, not we, who made the garden grow in your hearts. The person who does the planting or watering isn't important, but God is important because he is the one who makes things grow. Apollos and I are working as a team, with the same aim, though each of us will be rewarded for his own hard work. We are only God's co-workers. You are God's garden, not ours; you are God's building, not ours."*

Dan thought about George, Diane and the rest who received his messages. He thought how they felt in *Come Listen To Me*. Had the seed grown and flourished into a garden inside them, too? And, perhaps, the rest? "Yes," he asserted, as certain as his faith. "*Strange as it seems, we Christians actually have within us a portion of the very thoughts and mind of Christ.*" So Apostle Paul was talking about them and their garden.

Dan also understood what Apostle Paul meant when he said, "*We use Holy Spirit words to explain the Holy Spirit facts.* He knew these *words* are the characters of the Spirit that he reads in nature. They are about these facts: consistent, beautiful, precise, purposeful and so on. (Again the map and the territory sort of thing. For instance, the roots and leaves of a tree do their jobs purposefully and consistently to help make a tree realizes its own purpose. Its purpose is also consistently carried out. The distinction between the words and the facts are very subtle.)

Dan went back to the Great Equation. While he knew that God is the only one who could make it work, he also knew that, although we will always fall short on facts to make it work, we do possess enough tools to work with. We have the prophesies, visions and dreams of the wise men, including Jesus, to guide us in our conduct of life. We also have the common sense and a logical mind to understand. But, most importantly, we have the knowledge that God had put into our hearts, which we would know instinctively if we are attuned to the rhyme and reason of Nature, whose Spirit Jesus (the man) had.

Dan believed this is the reason Jesus came to us in the form of a man. He felt like us and subject to temptations and other weaknesses like us, including the most dreaded—the fear of death. He came to show us the way to win over them. So Dan thought that he would carry on the mission to spread the Word about Jesus:

1. That his purpose in life was to show us the Way to attain the Good Heart.

2. That in this heart lay Mercy and Love, the ultimate spiritual virtue.

3. That to make our hearts pure or sinless, we must be devoid of the passions of the Ego. (Jesus was a humble man.)

4. That to achieve this we must feed our souls with the "food for the soul"—by attuning them to the spirituality of Nature; that this is the way to emotional and mental discipline; and that this is the way to self-understanding and self-mastery.

5. That he would make a perfect model.

Now we understand. So we could be "forgiven." So we could be the image that our Creator had meant all of us to be.
Dan named his thoughts the "13th Man" and saved it.

* * * *

A message came in from Justin, the preacher:

Well—it's me again. I appreciate your sending me copies of your correspondences.

But you criticize the use of statues, prayers, the Holy Bible as a spiritual source and—most important of all—the Holy Name of Jesus. What are you an Anti-Christ?

Dan's reply:

Am I? Well, let's see. But first, let me get one thing straight. What do we mean "Anti-Christ"? Let me start with 1 John 22, where it says: *An Anti-Christ is one who says that Jesus is not Christ. Such a person is antichrist, for he does not believe in God the Father and in his Son.*

Now, who was Christ? Christ, as described in the dictionary, means 1. The Messiah whose appearance is prophesied in the Old Testament 2. Jesus of Nazareth, regarded by Christians as the realization of the Messianic prophecy.

Jesus was the one. One of his apostles said so, too. *From Matthew 16: 13-16: Jesus asked his disciples, "Who are the people saying I am?"*

"Well,' they replied, "some say John the Baptist; some Elijah; some, Jeremiah or one of the other prophets."

Then he asked them, "Who do you think I am?"

Simon Peter answered, "The Christ, the Messiah, the Son of the living God."

"God has blessed you, Simon, son of Jonah," Jesus said, "for my Father in heaven has personally revealed this to you—this is not from any human source."

So Jesus is Christ. Now, the next logical question is how do I know I am not an antichrist or I am for Christ? (I use the word "logical" the way Jesus used it, or—as the dictionary says—as "that follows as reasonable.")

Again, from 1 John, Apostle John said: *"Christ was alive when the world began, yet I myself have seen him with my own eyes and listened to him speak. I have touched him with my own hands. He is God's message of Life. He was with the Father and then was shown to us. Again I say, we are telling you about what we ourselves have actually seen and heard, so that you may share the fellowship and the joys we have with the Father and with Jesus Christ his Son."*

So announced the Christ, Messiah and the Son of the living God: *"I am the A and the Z, the beginning and the end. I have come onto the world to give sight to those who are spiritually blind and to show those who think they see that they are blind. They look but don't see, they hear but don't understand. I will send you the Comforter—the Holy Spirit—the source of all Truth. He will come to you from the Father and will tell you about me. No one can come to me unless the Father attracts them to me. For the truth about God is known to you instinctively. God had put this knowledge in your heart."*

Now, let's pick out a few of his statements and clarify them with examples and then compare them to see their effects to you and me.

A. *This is not from any human source.* To give you an example of a human source, I'll quote a letter by the prophet Jeremiah. He sent it to the Jews who were to be led captives into Babylon, to tell them of the instructions God gave him. It warned them against gods of gold, silver, stone or wood—the human source. It compared them against the natural things as to their effect on the soul.

Quote:
"Because of the sins that you have committed before God, you are to be taken as captives to Babylon by Nebuchadnezzar, king of Babylon. You will have to spend many years in Babylon, as much as seven generations. After that captivity, I will bring you home in peace. In Babylon, you will see gods of gold, silver, stone, and wood, carried about upon shoulders, bringing fear to the pagans. Be careful, therefore, that you do not imitate these pagan acts, nor should you be afraid of pagan gods, When you see the crowds pressing around the images and adoring them, you must say in your hearts, 'You alone must be adored, O Lord.' For my angel is with you, and I myself will demand an account of your souls. Plated with gold and silver, their tongues polished by artisans, they are only make-believe, unable to speak. Yet these gods cannot protect themselves from tarnish or decay, although they have been dressed in purple garments; they cannot even clean from themselves the temple dust which falls on them. One god holds a scepter, like a judge of the country, yet he is powerless to condemn an offender to death. Therefore do not fear them because they are only

powerless idols. Everything about these gods is fake. Therefore, it is better to be a king who shows his power, or even useful pot in a house with which the owner is satisfied, or a protective door to the house, than to be such false gods.

The sun, moon and stars shine usefully and obey God's laws. Lightning flashes across the sky. The winds blow over all nations. The clouds obey God's law and pass over the earth. Fire, which God created, burns woods and mountainsides as it was ordained to do. All these are more glorious and powerful than man-made gods. So no one has the right to think or say these idols are gods, since they can neither think or judge or do any good for mankind. These gods of wood, overlaid with gold and silver, are like a corpse hidden in the dark. In the end they will destroy themselves and a rebuke to their country. Better, therefore, is a good man with no idols; he will never suffer rebuke." This letter is comparing man-made things against natural things as to their effects.

(Let me say here that I consider prayers, name-callings and such as rituals. Do I do these things? Yes. I pray but not in front of any god of wood or metal or stone. And then I only do it after I have absorbed nature, like the beauty and the silence of the sun's radiance through the leaves or the beauty and silence of the night sky. I enjoy these things. I don't recall ever feeling this way when I prayed before idols.)

Now, let's look at the rest of the statements:

B. *"I am the A and the Z, the beginning and the end. I have come onto the world to give sight to those who are spiritually blind and to show those who think they see that they are blind. They look but don't see, they hear but don't understand. I will send you the Comforter—the Holy Spirit—the source of all Truth. He will come to you from the Father and will tell you about me. No one can come to me unless the Father attracts them to me. For the truth about God is known to you instinctively. God had put this knowledge in your heart."*

Now, let's compare it with this line from the 23rd Psalm:

"Because the Lord is my Shepherd, I have everything I need! He lets me rest in the meadow grass and leads me beside the quiet streams. He restores my failing health. He helps me do what honors him the most.

Even when waling through the dark valley of death I will not be afraid, for you are close beside me, guarding, guiding all the way.

You provide delicious food for me in the presence of my enemies. You have welcomed me as your guest; blessings overflow!

Your goodness and unfailing kindness shall be with me all of my life, and afterwards. I will live with you forever in your home."

Question: Do you feel the *comfort*? Don't you think this is the Comforter or the Holy Spirit Jesus is talking about in B? Do you feel the same way with the "idols"? Why feel? you may ask. Because this business of the Spirit is a basic feeling deep in the heart. It's in the *inmost self*. This feeling is what young Jesus sought after in the wilderness. The Bible calls it the Holy Spirit. *"As a boy, he was led by the Holy Spirit into the wilderness. He loved God so much he spent a lot of time there."*

Further, let me quote a poem by Corinne Roosevelt Robinson, *The Path That Leads To Nowhere*.

*There's a Path that leads to Nowhere
In a meadow that I know,
Where an inland river rises
And the stream is still and slow;
There it wanders under willows
And beneath the silver green
Of birches silent shadows
Where the early violets lean.*

Other pathways lead to Somewhere,

But the one I love so well
Had no end and no beginning—
Just the beauty of the dell,
Just the wildflowers and the lilies....

There I go to meet in the Springtime,
When the meadow is aglow'
Marigold amid the marshes,
And the stream is still and slow....

All the ways that lead to Somewhere
Echo with the hurrying feet
Of the struggling and the Striving,
But the way I find so sweet
Bids me dream and bids me linger–

Joy and Beauty are its goal;
On the path that leads to Nowhere
I have sometimes found my soul.

Now, isn't the substance in this poem the same as that in the 23rd Psalm? If so, then it is also the same substance as that in the statements made by Jesus in B regarding the *Comforter* or the *Holy Spirit*. To get this meaning more clearly, refer to the side-by-side comparison I made between Jesus statements and the description of my own experience. And to get the *real feel*, I suggest you do the same thing Diane did with *Come, Listen To Me*. Sit before a tree and read it. See if you think and feel the same way as you would with the idols. Now, which one is fake? Who sits or kneels before idols? Who is the Anti-Christ?

This Idolatry extends to the modern age, on the TV, movie, in books and magazines. We glue our eyes on them—from the blatant to the subtle (like the ads using Nature as a backdrop). We respond to them (sometimes to the extremes). We have fattened up (but not in our souls) and made our hearts even more disobedient. *Are we ashame we worship idols? No, not the least: we don't even know how to blush!* But let's be aware of these idolatries, these subtle manipulators, I say, lest they carry us away. Rather, let's tune in to the words of wisdom in nature once in a while.

"*A wise man's heart leads him to do right, and a fool's heart leads him to do evil.*

The heavens are made beautiful by the spirit who gives intuition and instinct. Who is wise enough to number the stars? They do not know where to find wisdom but death and destruction knows something about it. It is not age that makes man wise. Rather, it is the Spirit in man, the breath of the almighty which makes him intelligent. God had put this knowledge into their hearts."

God made us in his own image, intelligent and wise in his ways. He wants us to redeem this image. Jesus, his Son and the Great Teacher, showed us the *way*. Let's get this basic feeling, the *Comforter*, in our hearts. Let's understand ourselves as we understand Him, lest self-destruction or destruction overtakes us.

I enjoyed talking to you. I look forward to hearing from you again.

Your friend,

Dan

Chapter 16

Dan and Buster missed Betty. Now they do the chore she left, not the least of which were the meals and the dishes. They also host the visitors.

Kids, with their parents' permission, were brought over by their teachers to see the place. They love the chickens and the birds. They enjoyed watching the birds drink and wash themselves.

Dan would give a talk about the plants (although not as a horticulturist or a botanist or even a gardener). Sometimes he would hint at a Higher Being, saying that there is a purpose for every little thing that makes up a plant which, in turn, has its own purpose for being, contributing to the whole and synchronizing with the rest of creation to make a harmonious Whole. They all bow to this Higher Being. But he would not go any farther than that. He wouldn't tell the teachers that Jesus was the only who had *seen* this *Being*. He thought he would scare the dickens out of them.

"Come see us again," Dan would say when they left, although he had a feeling they wouldn't come back.

* * * *

Dan would rather tell his visitors that: *God's Kingdom is in the heart…He had put this knowledge in the heart…We know these things are true by believing not by seeing…It is the thought-life that pollutes. For from within, out of men's hearts, come evil thoughts of lust, theft, murder, adultery, wickedness, deceit, envy, lewdness, slander, pride, and all other folly…To forsake evil is true understanding…It is the Spirit in man that makes him wise…*and so on; that this is the essence of Jesus' New Covenant and that a garden is *the* place to start. But Dan knew they couldn't care any less about this kind of talk.

They wouldn't understand just like the Jews did not understand. The Jews wouldn't understand even when God had poured his wrath upon them for being stubborn and rebellious. They refused to move away from the Old Covenant—the system of laws, idols and blood rituals—to the new one, for there remained this veil of misunderstanding that covered their hearts and minds.

Dan read an episode in the Bible that illustrates this. He studied it to see if he could learn something that might help him convince and educate his listeners. The episode went:

Jesus told them: "I am telling you what I saw when I was with my Father. But you are following the advice of your father.

"Our father is Abraham," they declared.

"No!" Jesus replied, "for if he were, you would follow his good example. But instead you are trying to kill me—and all because I told you the truth I heard from God. Abraham wouldn't do a thing like that! No, you are obeying your real father when you act that way."

They replied, "We were not born out of wedlock—our true Father is God himself."

Jesus told them, "If that were so, then you would love me, for I have come to you from God. I am not here on my own, but he sent me. Why can't you understand what I am saying? It is because you are prevented from doing so! For you are the children of your father the devil and you love to do evil things he does. He was a murderer from the beginning and a hater of truth—there is not an iota of truth in him. When he lies, it is perfectly normal; for he is the father of liars. And so when I tell the truth, you just naturally don't believe it!

"Which of you can truthfully accuse me of one single sin? And since I am telling you the truth, why don't you believe me? Anyone whose Father is God listens gladly to the words of God. Since you don't, it proves you aren't his children."

"You Samaritan! Foreigner! Devil!" the Jewish leaders snarled. "Didn't we say all along you were possessed by a demon?"

"No," Jesus said, "I have no demons in me. For I honor my Father—and you dishonor me. And though I have no wish to make myself great, God wants this for me and judges. With all the earnestness I have I tell you this—no one who obeys me shall ever die!" (Dan paused at this point and considered the last line: "*…no one who obeys me shall ever die.*" He recalled that Jesus said something to this effect when he was being tempted by Satan. He told the Satan he only *obeyed God and that obedience to every of God* was what he needed. He was not doomed to die because he obeyed every word of God. But Adam and Eve were doomed to die because they disobeyed God when they ate the forbidden fruit. Jesus regained the lost Spirit. He was, is and will be. He was the Spirit. God sent him as a man to give mankind a second chance to redeem himself and live the eternal life. He was the *Redeemer*.)

Dan continued reading and interpreting. *The leaders of the Jews said, "Now we know you are possessed by a demon. Even Abraham and mightiest prophets died, and yet you say that obeying you will keep a man from dying! So you are greater than our Father Abraham, who died? And greater than the prophets who died? Who do you think you are?" Then Jesus told them this: "If I am merely boasting about myself, it doesn't count. But it is my Father—and you claim him as your God—who is saying these glorious things about me. But you do not even know him. I do. If I said otherwise, I would be as great a liar as you! But it is true—I know him and fully obey* him. Your father Abraham rejoiced to see my day. He knew I was coming and was glad."

The Jewish leaders: "You aren't even fifty years old—sure, you've seen Abraham!"

Jesus: "The absolute truth is that I was in existence before Abraham was ever born!" (Logically, Dan thought this statement means the same thing when Jesus said (referring to himself as the son of God and the Spirit), "I am the A and the Z, the beginning and the end.")

At that point the Jewish leaders picked up stones to kill him. But Jesus was hidden from them and walked past them and left the temple.

As he was walking along, he saw a man blind from birth.

"Master," his disciples asked him "why was this man born blind? Was it a result of his own sins or those of his parents?"

"Neither," Jesus answered. "But to demonstrate the power of God, all of us must quickly carry out the tasks assigned us by the one who sent me, for there is little time left before the night falls and all work comes to an end. But while I am still here in the world, I give my light."

Then he spat on the ground and made from the spittle and smoothed the mud over the blind man's eyes, and told him "Go and wash in the Pool of Siloam." So the man went where he was sent and came back seeing!

His neighbors and others who knew him as a blind beggar asked each other, "Is this the same fellow—that beggar?"

Some said yes, and some said no. "It can't be the same man," they thought, "but he surely looks like him!"

And the beggar said, "I am the same man!"

Then they asked him how in the world he could see. What had happened?

And he told them, "A man they call Jesus made mud and smoothed it over my eyes and told me to go to the Pool of Siloam and wash off the mud. I did, and I can see!"

"Where is he now?" they asked.

"I don't know," he replied.

Then they took the man to the Pharisees. Now as it happened, this all occurred on Sabbath. Then the Pharisees asked him all about it. So he told them how Jesus had smoothed the mud over his eyes, and when it was washed away, he could see!

Some of them said, "Then this fellow Jesus is not from God, because he is working on the Sabbath."

Others said, "But how could an ordinary sinner do such miracles?" So there was a deep division of opinion among them.

Then the Pharisees turned on the man who had been blind and demanded, "This man who opened your eyes—who do you say he is?"

"I think he must be a prophet sent from God," the man replied.

The Jewish leaders wouldn't believe he had been blind, until they called his parents and asked them, "Is this your son?"

His parents replied, "We know this is our son and that he was born blind, but we don't know what happened to him see, or who did it. He is old enough to speak for himself. Ask him."

They said this in fear of the Jewish leaders who had announced that anyone saying Jesus was the Messiah would be excommunicated.

So for the second time they called in the man who had been blind and told him, "Give the glory to God, not to Jesus, for we know Jesus is an evil person."

"I don't know whether he is good or bad," the man replied, "but I know this: I was blind, and now I see!"

"But what did he do?" they asked. "How did he heal you?"

"Look!" the man exclaimed. "I told you once; you didn't listen? Why do you want to hear it again? Do you want to become his disciples too?"

Then they cursed him and said, "You are his disciple, but we are the disciples of Moses. We know God has spoken to Moses, but as for this fellow, we don't know anything about him."

Why, that's very strange the man replied. "He can heal blind men, and yet you don't know anything about him! Well, God doesn't listen to evil men, but he has open ears to those who worship him and do his will. Since the world began there has never been anyone who could open the eyes of someone born blind. If this man were not from God, he couldn't do it."

You illegitimate bastard, you!" they shouted. "Are you trying to teach us? And they threw him out.

When Jesus heard what had happened, he found the man and said, "Do you believe in the Messiah?"

The man answered, "Who is he, sir, for I want to."

"You have seen him," Jesus said, "and he is speaking to you!"

"Yes, Lord," the man said, "I believe!" And he worshiped Jesus.

Then Jesus told him, "I have come into the world to give sight to those who are spiritually blind and to show those who think they see that they are blind."

The Pharisees who were standing there asked, "Are you saying we are blind?"

"If you were blind, you wouldn't be guilty," Jesus replied. "But your guilt remains because you claim to know what you are doing."

*   *   *   *

The Pharisees just didn't understand Jesus. They were not convinced that he was the Spirit, the son of God, but sent to them as a man. Neither truth nor miracle could make a dent in the people's minds. So Dan wondered: If Jesus couldn't convince them, how could he? He wondered how to present his understanding.

But first, Dan studied the Old Covenant. It went:

The OLD SYSTEM of Jewish laws gave only a dim foretaste of the good things Christ would do for the Jews. The sacrifices under the old system were repeated again and again, year after year, but even so they could never save those who lived under their rules. If they could have, one offering would have been enough; the worshipers would have been cleansed one for all, and their feeling of guilt would be gone. (This guilt thing reminded Dan of George's guilt feelings.)

But just the opposite happened: those yearly sacrifices reminded them of their disobedience and guilt instead of relieving their minds. For it is not possible for the blood of bulls and goats really to take way sins. (Dan asked: If blood of bulls and goats couldn't do it, how about confessions, communions and praying before idols that people do today?)

So the need for the New Covenant. Dan continued reading.

Death and destruction did not seem to change the old one. It seemed the only option left for God was send his Son Jesus. He empowered him with himself. He made him God.

He came as a man. God gave him the title of a High Priest. As a High Priest he understood their weaknesses, since he had the same temptations they had, though he never once gave way to them and sinned. Even though he was God's Son, he had to learn from experience what it was like to obey, when obeying meant suffering; for his suffering made Jesus a perfect Leader, one fit to bring them into their salvation. (This part reminded Dan of Jesus' statements he made when he was suffering during his crucifixion: "Father," he said, *"if you are willing, please take away this cup of horror from me. But I want your will not mine…The spirit indeed is willing, but how weak the body is!"* Earlier, he told his disciples to keep alert and pray, otherwise temptation will overpower them. Here, Dan was reminded of an advice: Be strong. Yes, be very strong.)

Dan continued reading: *Since we, God's children, are human beings—made of flesh and blood—he became flesh and blood too by being born in human form; for only as a human being could he die and in dying break the power of the devil who had the power of death. Only in that way could he deliver those who through fear of death have been living all their lives as slaves to constant dread.* (On this one, Dan thought that Jesus, as a human, he felt fear, too. He realized that fear, of all the emotions, is the biggest barrier to total freedom. But he also knew that Jesus knew that *fear is nothing but the surrender of reason,* so that what Jesus was saying is that you have nothing to fear if you are not afraid even of death. He was a Platonic or a stoic. So then the devil could not enslave him with his power, which is fear. Dan knew this from the Book of

Psalm, where it said: "*He leadeth me by the still water. He comforteth me. Even when walking through the dark valley of death I will not be afraid, for you are close beside me, guarding, guiding all the way.*" Dan knew Jesus knew this.)

Dan continued to read and interpret. *Jesus cancelled the old covenant or system in favor of a far better one. Under this new plan they have been forgiven and made clean by Christ's dying for them once and for all.* (Dan paused and considered this statement. He was in a quandary, as if he were at the fork of a road. But he recalled the 23rd Psalm and the phrase "…*for his suffering made Jesus a perfect leader.*" Dan thought that by suffering and dying, Jesus was being obedient to his mission as the Messiah. He obeyed to the point of death, fearlessly. This made him a perfect leader. He *leadeth us by the still water,* for the fear of death is too much for us ordinary mortals. Being a mortal human being himself, he understood and forgave us for our weaknesses.) *And the Holy Spirit testifies that this is so, for he has said:* "*This is the agreement I will make with the people of Israel, though they broke their first agreement: I will write my laws into their minds so that they will always know my will, and I will put my laws into their hearts so that they will want to obey them. I will never again remember their sins and lawless deeds.*" Now Dan felt he was back on the right track. What this means to him is that Jesus had planted the seed of the Spirit in man, a seed that may grow into a garden in him. Dan describes this Spirit as wisdom. He drew a passage from the Book of Wisdom:

"*The spirit of wisdom is benevolent, and will not free the evil speaker from his words. God is witness to his feelings, and a true searcher of his heart, and a hearer of his tongue.*"

The speaker uttered these words: "*Therefore I prayed and understanding was given me; I called upon God, and the spirit of wisdom came upon me. I preferred her to kingdoms and thrones, and esteemed riches as nothing in comparison to her. I loved her above health and beauty, and chose to have her instead of light; for her light cannot be put out. Now all good things came to me along with her, and innumerable riches through her hands, and I rejoiced in all these; for this wisdom went before me, and I did not know that she was the mother of them all. I have learned without guile, communicate without envy, and do not hide her riches. For in her is the spirit of understanding: holy, unique, many-faceted, subtle eloquent, active, undefiled, sure, sweet, loving, good, quick, irresistible. And if a man desires much knowledge, she knows things past and foretells what is to come; she knows the subtleties of speeches, and the solutions of arguments; she knows signs and wonders before they are done, and the outcome of ages. For she is an infinite treasure to men, who, if they use it, become the friends of God, being commended for the gift of discipline."*

Discipline. Self-control. Dan thought these virtues helped George get rid of his guilt feeling. It helped him, too, and Julius, Buster and Betty and perhaps many others. Dan talked about them with the visitors. He told them that the silence, peace and beauty of nature teach mental and emotional discipline, and that in his book *The Will to Doubt,* Mathematician-Philosopher Bertrand Russell said: "Discipline is best when it springs from inner impulse...Even self-discipline depends, in the end, upon educational stimulus." Dan believes there could be no better educational stimulus than the spirituality of nature. The teachers got the message. They loved it. This, essentially, is the crux of Jesus New Covenant. *"I will write my laws into their minds so that they will always know my will, and I will put my laws into their hearts so that the will want to obey them. I will never again remember sins and lawless deeds."*

Dan saved his thoughts and sent them out to all his correspondents.

* * * *

A question was sent in by Dale of Canada. He said: I have this message from a friend who mentioned you and your website forum. He said that in one of your discussions you said that only Jesus had *seen* God. What do you mean? Is God something like an image that we can see with our own eyes?

Dan's reply:

Thank you, Dale, for your interest in my discussions. Here's my response to your question:

God made man in his image. What is the image? Before I try to give you an answer, let me point out that the image is usually not what we see around us, or the image that others might want us to think or have.

According to Apostle Paul, only Jesus had *seen* God. By "God made man in his image," I believe the image is this: Man has an ordered mind and a heart that carries the Spirit. By well-ordered mind, I mean the mind described by Plato, the Greek philosopher of old. The description is this:

> "Beauty depends on simplicity—I mean true simplicity
> of a rightly ordered mind and character.
> He is a fool who seriously inclines to weigh the beautiful
> by any other standard than that of the good.
> The good is beautiful.
> Grant me to be beautiful in the inner man."

Simplicity. Beauty. The Good. Rightly ordered mind and character.Spirit. This, then, is the image God made man to be. Let's take a closer look at this image. Let's look at a leaf, for example. The dictionary tells us that a leaf is "any flat, thin, expanded organ, usually green, growing laterally from the stem or twig of a plant." This describes what we see. But what about that we don't see? What happens to its design after it falls off and disappears into earth? Let's assume the leaf was designed after a perfect circle. Did this perfect "circleness" die, too? We imagine not. It remains intact regardless of the physical condition of its earthly image. So this circle leaf is an image of the perfect circle. Now, let's go from here and say that we are created in the image of God. Just as the leaf is designed and created as a working part of the whole tree, so we are created as a working part of a greater whole. Its design and function is, let's say, its Spirit. Likewise, our design and function is our

Spirit, that in the image of God or molded after a perfect Being we call "God." But now let's ask, are we functioning with the Spirit in us like we are supposed to? Like a leaf does? No—not until we obey, as Jesus said. We are not a leaf without choice. We are given the choice. It's up to us to obey or not.

Also, around the time of Plato, the Greek Stoics "chose spots of great beauty in which to build shrines to the healing gods. These were described as "places where the whole of the universe of men and nature come together in a single quiet order to be healed."

To be "healed," Jesus, the small boy, *went to the wilderness. He loved God so much he spent a lot of time there before he began his ministry.* In other words, he went to the wilderness because he loved the peace and beauty, the birds and the trees, the flowers and the bees and so on. He *saw* in them the work of a well-ordered mind and character. He *saw* the image of God: Simplicity. Beauty. The Good. They became his Spirit as well. He became *the* Spirit. "*I am in the Father and the Father is in me,*" he said later on in his life.

"*In order to understand the Spirit, one must have the Spirit first. Those who have the Holy Spirit in them can understand what the Holy Spirit means then use the Holy Spirit words to explain the Holy Spirit facts. And in order for one to be called a Christian, he must have the same Spirit Jesus had.*' You have this Spirit and you have the image of God. We can only imagine the image of God. We can only imagine the image of a perfect circle or express it only in a mathematical formula. But, according to Apostle Paul, only Jesus had seen God. He did because he was, is and will always be as perfect as him.

I hope I make sense. I am also sending you my other correspondences. Please pass the word around.

Sincerely,

Dan

Chapter 17

Julius called Dan to ask if he could join them. He said he could cook. But most of all he said he wanted to be with them and study with them.

Dan knew that Julius had *the beginning of wisdom which is the most sincere desire for instruction* (or the most sincere desire for instruction is the beginning of wisdom). Dan told him he'd call him right back. He wanted to check with George first, just for courtesy's sake. George said that would be great. Dan called Julius right away.

"It's fine with us," Dan said. "We'd love to try your cooking."

Julius wasn't only a good cook, he was also a handyman. He fixed the lawnmower and the sprinklers that day. When he was done, he went to buy grocery which he paid with his own money, and that evening he cooked.

"Hmmm-mm! This is real soul-food!" Buster said, relishing the sweet mashed potato, beans and pork ribs barbecued Southern style. "Where'd ya learn all this?" he asked.

"A friend. He invited me to his house." Julius said.

"This is delicious, indeed," Dan said. "Did you learn this in school, I mean–cooking?"

"Yes—as a matter of fact," Julius said. "After I got my GED, I went to school a bit. Now I work as short order cook."

"You're goin' to spoil us," Dan said, smiling.

"He's got me," Buster said. "I'll eat any leftover tonight—if I don't finish it all right now." Buster didn't really mean it. He was only showing his appreciation. He liked Julius. Julius liked him, too.

Dan liked Julius, too. What a turn-around he made of his life, he thought—from being self-destructive or destructive to constructive, from bad to good.

* * * *

Julius had the Bible that Betty left in her room. He started reading it.

Julius asked Dan what the following verses meant:

1) *The heart is deceitful above all things, and desperately wicked: who can know?*

2) *As it is written, there is none righteous, no, not one. There is none that understandeth, there is none that seeketh after God. They are all gone out of the way, they are together become unprofitable; there is none that doeth good, no, not one."*

3) *For the Son of man is come to save that which was lost.*

Dan gave his answers in printed form. The reason is that he wanted Julius to take his time to study it. His answers:

"Answer to 1: Jesus knew. He said: *"It is the thought—life that pollutes. For from within, out of men's hearts, come evil thoughts of lust, theft, murder, adultery, wickedness, deceit, envy, lewdness, slander, pride, and all other folly."*

Who else can know it? God, and possibly you. *"God knows our hearts. For whatever God says to us is full of living power: it is sharper than the sharpest dagger, cutting swift and deep into our innermost thoughts and desires with all their parts, exposing us for what we really are. I hope that, deep within you, you really know it too. Cleanse your mind and heart."*

The answer to 2 is found in question 3. Again, it is Jesus who knew. *"He is righteous, understanding and seeketh God. He doeth good.* He also said: *"I will reveal secrets since the beginning of time."* One of these secrets is the solution to the human folly or stupidity.

Apostle Paul also told about this solution when he said: *"I advise you to obey only the Holy Spirit's instructions. He will tell you where to go and what to do, and then you won't always be doing the wrong things your evil nature wants you to. For we naturally love to do evil things that the Holy Spirit tells us to do; and the good things we want to do when the Spirit has his way with us are just the opposite of your natural desires. These two forces within us are constantly fighting each other to win control over us, and our wishes are never free from their pressures. When you area guided by the Holy Spirit you need no longer force yourself to obey Jewish laws.*

But when you follow your own wrong inclinations your lives will produce these evil results: impure thoughts, eagerness for lustful pleasure, idolatry, spiritism (that is encouraging the activity of demons), hatred and fighting, jealousy and anger, constant effort to get the best for yourself, complaints and criticisms, feeling that everyone else is wrong except those in your own little group—and there will be wrong doctrine, envy, murder, drunkenness, wild parties, and all that sort of thing. Let me tell you again as I have before, that anyone living that sort of life will not inherit the kingdom of God.

But when the Holy Spirit controls our lives he will produce this kind of fruit in us: love joy, peace, patience, kindness, goodness, faithfulness, gentleness and self-control.

Those who belong to Christ have nailed their natural desires to his cross and crucified them there.

If we are living now by the Holy Spirit's power, let us follow the Holy Spirit's leading in every part of our lives. Then we won't need to look for honors and popularity, which lead to jealousy and hard feelings."

This is the long and the short of the solution. Jesus wanted us is to obey and follow this instruction. What's so curious is that man just couldn't seem to learn to obey. He's just plain foolish. He knows nothing about his foolishness and he loves it. Jesus knows all about it and he hates it. One wonders what he's going do next.

Julius, you asked *where the good road is, the godly paths you used to walk in, in the days of long ago. Travel there, and you'll find rest for your soul.* You took the first steps. You're traveling there right now. You found the long-hidden road.

As usual, Dan saved Julius questions and his answers. He saved it as "Julius" then sent it out.

* * * *

Buster and Julius visited and helped the homeless around Las Vegas. Sometimes, they would bring home a few of them. Some of them got into this plight because of social security red tape while others were just plain broke after losing their jobs and their families. Julius would drive them to where they could get the help they needed. They appreciated the help. Sometimes they get curious about their place. They answer them matter-of-factly. They did not want to make them feel indebted to them. But they gave them copies of all their correspondences when they left.

They visited the home-bound elderlies. They gave them their phone and fax numbers to contact them if they needed help. Buster used to be the arbiter-peacemaker in jail. He volunteered with the police. At night, he would ride patrol with them. Surprised teens and men hanging around in street corners obeyed him—or were scared of him. He became a regular member of the Inn. In time, he organized groups to patrol their own neighborhood at night. It worked. Their streets became safer. He was encouraged to run for County Sheriff but he turned it down. He didn't want the job, besides he didn't think he could win anyway, being a convicted felon he once was. He'd rather take care of peoples' souls, he said. Toward this end, he dedicated his life. So did Julius. They stayed on with Dan, who kept on speaking.

Because of the power of the internet, his Word had reached far and wide like ripples on a pond reaching its shores.

* * * *

Dan received the news that Betty was going to have a baby. The doctor said he is a boy. George was excited and started preparing for his arrival.

Several months after their child's birth, George sent for Dan, Buster and Julius for the baptism. They named their son "Bobby." The ceremony was a simple one. It was held at the same chapel where they were married. George took them out on his yacht for a day cruise to Victoria, B.C.. Again, they enjoyed the same Pacific Northwest fare.

* * * *

As Bobby grew up, he looked more and more like his uncle. His face, particularly his eyes, were his uncle's. God! George gasped, as he looked into his son's eyes one day. A deep, indescribable feeling surged in him. He was looking at his very own brother! He shared his excitement with everybody. Bobby was a God-send.

Chapter 18

▼

"George, turn your TV on!" shouted Dan excitedly over the phone, as he watched wide-eyed in horror at two New York skyscrapers, getting hit by jet planes, first one and then the other, then another one did the same thing with the Pentagon, yet another plunged into a wreckage on a cornfield in Pennsylvania. He watched the two tall buildings collapsed into huge balls of dust that rolled down the city street, chasing an exodus of dust-covered and startled men and women. Sirens wailed. The city turned into a pandemonium. America was under attack! He felt like somebody has barged into his home. He felt angry and helpless. The specter was the work of terrorists.

"Oh, my God!" George gasped. Sitting next to him was his now two-something Bobby. He picked him up and set him on his lap. "Honey, Come here!" he called out. Betty was in the kitchen helping out.

"Oh, my God!" Betty exclaimed in horror. She huddled closer to George and Bobby. "How could this happen? Why?" She asked. They watched. The scene came on over and over.

"Why?" George asked, calmly. Perhaps thinking that his dad was talking to him, Bobby looked up at him, as if he was asking the same question. The way he looked reminded George of an e-mail Dan sent him. He handed Bobby to Betty and went to his computer. He pulled out a copy and went back to join Betty and Bobby. He read:

Dear Dan,

Could you give me examples of prophesies and actual events that correspond to them? Also, could you give me an example of history repeating itself?

Thank you.

Jen

I like your questions, Jen. Here are some examples:

Prophesies (This one came from Isaiah.): *"For unto us a Child is born; unto us a Son is given; and the government shall be upon his shoulder. These will be his royal titles: Wonderful, Counselor, The Mighty God, The Everlasting Father, The Prince of Peace. His government was upon his shoulder.* He would be made to suffer and die.

The other prophecy came from the Book of Daniel: *Then I, Daniel, looked and saw two men on each bank of a river. And one of them asked the man in a linen robe who was standing now above the water, "How long will it be until all terrors end?"*

He replied with both hands lifted to heaven, taking oath by him who lives forever and ever, that they will not end until three and a half years after the power of God's people are crushed.

I heard what he said but I didn't understand what he meant, so I said, "Sir, how will this all come out?"

But he said, "Go now, Daniel, for what I have said is not to be understood until the time of the end. Many shall be purified by great trials and persecutions. But the wicked shall continue in their wickedness, and none of them will understand. It will not be understood until the end times, when travel and education shall be vastly increased. And even then only those who are willing to learn will know what it means." Guess who the man in the white robe was? It was Jesus.

History repeating itself: (This also came from Isaiah.) "*Woe to Jerusalem, the city of David. Year after year you make your many offerings, but I will send heavy judgment upon you and there will be weeping and sorrow. For Jerusalem shall become as her name "Ariel" means—an altar covered with blood. I will be your enemy. I will surround Jerusalem and lay siege against it, and build forts around it to destroy it.*

Your voice will whisper like a ghost from the earth where you lie buried.

But suddenly your ruthless enemies will be driven away like chaff before the wind. In an instant, I the Lord of Hosts, will come upon them with thunder, earthquake, whirlwind and fire. And all the nations fighting Jerusalem will vanish like a dream!

You are amazed, incredulous? You don't believe it? Then go ahead and be blind if you must! You are stupid—and not from drinking, either! Stagger, and not from wine. For the Lord has poured out upon you a spirit of deep sleep. He has closed the eyes of your prophets and seers, so all these future events are a sealed book to them."

What do think, Jen? Don't they sound like today's news? They are accurate almost to the point, aren't they?

It's a pleasure discussing with you. Would you help pass the word around?

Sincerely,

Dan

How amazing! George thought. Daniel's prophecy and history being repeated are incredibly uncanny. They were written a long time ago, and they are happening right now. Only a blind man wouldn't see how it fits the events in Israel, but George couldn't see how it fits the attack on the U.S. or us. Regardless, it is upon us all, he reasoned. We are attacked for whatever reason they might have. He turned the events and prophecy over and over in his mind trying to find a reason or meaning when out of the depth of recent history, the haunting memory of the Unknown Soldier came to him. He wondered: Who was this young man? What did he die for? Did he die for the love of his country and its principles? Did he die for the land—the beautiful meadows, lakes, rivers, mountains and valleys? His memory traveled through the wars America fought: From the early Indian Wars, to the Civil War, to World Wars 1 and 2, to the Vietnam War and to all the wars in between. Which war did the Unknown Soldier fight in? It could be in any one of them, he thought. The soldier knew America is not perfect and never will be. But he also knew his people would keep striving towards its ideals, those written in its own Book of the Future. George knew that, too. He recalled a book he read, the one written by an early Filipino immigrant, who was a migrant worker. He wrote:

"America is not a land of one race or one class of men. We are all Americans that have toiled and suffered and known oppression and defeat, from the first Indian that offered peace in Manhattan to the last Filipino pea pickers. America is not bound by geographical latitudes. America is not merely a land or an institution. America is in the hearts of men that died for freedom. It is also in the eyes of men that are building a new world. America is a prophecy of a new society of men: of a system that knows no sorrow or strife or suffering. America is a warning to those who would try to falsify the ideals of free men…"

George shared the author's feelings. They are fine sentiments of men, he thought; sentiments yet to be learned by us and the people spoken of by Daniel; the same sentiment of Abraham whose faith and obedience to God was tested by him. He was willing to give his beloved son Isaac to a sacrifice that was to prove it. This sentiment is in the heart. It is spiritual. His thoughts turned again to the Unknown Soldier, the beloved son of someone. He proved his spirituality—his love for his country—when he paid the ultimate price.

"There's the American proof—damn right, it is!" George said, loudly. He said it with so much heart it startled Bobby. He looked up at his dad, who looked down into his beautiful and innocent eyes. He saw in Bobby's eyes the meaning of all these: The Unknown Soldier helped wrote the Book of the Future for America. He wrote it for his son and for all the future sons and daughters of America so that they may live freely to prophesize, to dream dreams, to see visions and to love, to have faith and to have hope.

"Yes, the attackers and their sponsors are a bunch of fools," George thought. "They started out with a premise that will conclude in sheer madness and bring them ruins. They are falsifying our principles of Freedom and Liberty, principles borne out of our love of the land." George noted down his thoughts and sent it to Dan to send out for all to share. Dan sent it out along with this message:

To my fellow Americans: *Fear is nothing but the surrender of reason. Be strong. Yes, be very strong. In quietness and confidence is our strength. We will not fail.*

✶   ✶   ✶   ✶

"The Road Not Taken"
by Robert Frost

"Two roads diverged in a yellow wood,
And sorry I could not travel both
And be one traveler, long I stood
And looked down one as far as I could
To where it bent in the undergrowth…"

My Bio: I was born in the Philippines. At age seventeen, I joined and served in the United States Navy for six years. Soon After my discharge, I moved to Seattle, Washington where I attended college, became a real estate broker, got married and raised two sons.

My wife and I have retired and moved to Las Vegas where we keep a piece of Nature in our backyard.

My aim in writing *The Thirteenth Man*, as in *Where True Peace Lies*, is to spread my understanding about my connection with Nature, and how it helped me understand myself, my world and the most important man that ever lived: Jesus.

For more information on how I got started off on this road please visit:

www.wheretruepeacelies.org.

SOURCES

New World Dictionary Second College Edition

The Way The Living Bible (Tyndale House Publishers)

The Path That Leads to Nowhere Corinne Roosevelt Robinson

Who Loves a Garden Louise Seymour Jones

The Inner Man Best Loved Poems to Read Again and Again (Galahad Books)

America Is In the Heart Carlos Bulosan

Language In Thought And Action S. I. Hayakawa

Where True Peace Lies Rudy A. Pizarro (wheretruepeacelies.org.)

0-595-25765-8